## "Damn it, Jazz, if you want me out of here, just say so."

Instantly Adam wished he could take the words back. The expression on her face was a mixture of shock, hurt and something else he couldn't identify.

"Don't take it that way," she said quietly. "You must have better things to do than babysitting me and Iris."

"I ain't got one better thing to do than make sure you and your niece are safe. Period."

Jazz bit her lip and leaned back against the counter, forgoing her chair. "But it seems like such a small thing..."

"Really?" Adam asked harshly. *"Really?"*

After a few seconds, she shook her head. "No. It doesn't." She closed her eyes.

"Exactly. I don't think you're overreacting at all."

Jazz reached for her coffee. The mug was still warm, and the coffee felt good going down her throat. She wondered if she would ever feel warm again. Or completely unafraid...

# CONARD COUNTY: MISTAKEN IDENTITY

---

*New York Times* **Bestselling Author**

# RACHEL LEE

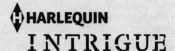

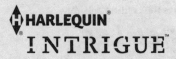

# HARLEQUIN®
# INTRIGUE™

PLEASE RECYCLE · THIS PRODUCT IS RECYCLABLE

Recycling programs for this product may not exist in your area.

ISBN-13: 978-1-335-48943-2

Conard County: Mistaken Identity

Harlequin Enterprises ULC
22 Adelaide St. West, 41st Floor
Toronto, Ontario M5H 4E3, Canada
www.Harlequin.com

**Printed in U.S.A.**

**Rachel Lee** was hooked on writing by the age of twelve and practiced her craft as she moved from place to place all over the United States. This *New York Times* bestselling author now resides in Florida and has the joy of writing full-time.

### Books by Rachel Lee

### Harlequin Intrigue

#### Conard County: The Next Generation

*Cornered in Conard County*
*Missing in Conard County*
*Murdered in Conard County*
*Conard County Justice*
*Conard County: Hard Proof*
*Conard County: Traces of Murder*
*Conard County: Christmas Bodyguard*
*Conard County: Mistaken Identity*

### Harlequin Romantic Suspense

#### Conard County: The Next Generation

*A Conard County Spy*
*Conard County Marine*
*Undercover in Conard County*
*Conard County Revenge*
*Conard County Watch*
*Stalked in Conard County*
*Hunted in Conard County*
*Conard County Conspiracy*

Visit the Author Profile page at Harlequin.com.

## CAST OF CHARACTERS

*Jasmine (Jazz) Nelson*—Lily's twin sister, who has come from Miami to Conard City to watch her twin's daughter for a few weeks. She allows people to mistake her for Lily.

*Adam Ryder*—A vet with an enduring injury and some PTSD who steps in to help Jazz when someone begins to stalk her.

*Lily Robbins*—Jazz's twin sister. Away in Europe on consulting business.

*Iris Robbins*—Lily's fifteen-year-old daughter. She wanted to stay home with all her friends, so Jazz takes care of her for Lily.

*Andy Robbins*—Lily's ex-husband. Fresh out of prison, he has a score to settle with Lily.

*Sheba*—Adam's Irish setter, a comfort dog.

# Chapter One

Jasmine Nelson picked up the phone to hear her twin sister's welcome voice.

"Hey, Jazz," Lily said. "How are you making out with Iris?"

Jazz smiled into the phone. For a fifteen-year-old, her niece was an easy kid to deal with. "We're doing fine. How's Stockholm?"

"As usual. Someday you'll have to come with me. I can attend conferences and meetings and you can take in the sights. There are a lot of good ones."

"I bet."

Just then Iris burst through the front door, an energetic girl with tightly curly red hair that was amenable to no brush and required a short cut to easily fit under her swim cap. Her hair also got curlier in the rain and sometimes frizzed. None of this bothered Iris in the least.

"Hey, Iris. Want to talk to your mom?"

Iris screwed up her face.

"Let me guess," Lily said. "I'm the last person on earth she wants to talk to."

"Only because you're her mom." Jazz laughed. "She treats me *ever* so much better."

Iris screwed up her face again, stuck out her tongue and headed for the kitchen with her backpack.

"So no problem," Lily said. "I hope that continues. I'll call again in a couple of days. And obviously you know how to reach me if Iris gets arrested."

"In *this* town? If she does anything that bad, I think the cops will bring her home and present her for house punishment."

It was Lily's turn to laugh. "You're probably right. So after only three days you've figured out Conard County?"

"Well, that's debatable, but I'm learning."

Lily made a kissie sound over the phone. "Later, sis."

Iris bounced back into the small foyer, a peanut butter sandwich in hand, bag in the other. "I got the mail," she said, tossing her backpack onto a nearby straight-backed chair. "I just threw out all the flyers. I don't know why Mom gets any mail anyway. She pays all the bills automatically."

Before Jazz could answer, Iris bent and pulled a slim stack of envelopes from her pack and tossed them into a basket on top of the envelopes that had begun to build up over the past few days. Jazz never looked at them, preserving Lily's privacy. Neither of them guessed there was a bombshell in that stack.

"I am so glad you're not twins," Jazz announced.

Iris giggled. "I've heard some of what you and Mom got up to. I could be double trouble."

She wasn't much of a problem to begin with, but Jazz didn't say so. No reason to encourage it. "I wish you'd talk with Lily next time she calls."

Iris shrugged. "She's the one who went to Stockholm."

"And you're the one who chose to stay here. What do I recall? Something about friends and school and swim team and oboe lessons."

Iris grinned. "Yeah, well."

"Well." Her niece always made Jazz smile. "What's the agenda?"

"I do my homework and you cook dinner."

"I knew you had it figured out. Why don't you help me cook?"

"Too much homework." With that, Iris vanished into the dining room with her backpack.

Jazz found it impossible to get annoyed with the girl. She was like a ray of sunshine coming through the door and she usually stayed that way all through homework, washing dishes and spending countless hours on her cell phone with her friends.

Nope. No problem. At least not yet.

Although Jazz wondered why Iris spent so many hours on the phone in the evenings. A teen thing?

Or that there was no good place for them to meet up? She had no idea. Maybe she should ask.

Iris poked her head out the dining room door. "Hey, Aunt Jazz?"

"Yes?"

"It's a good thing Grandma didn't have another set of twins. Can you imagine the names? Begonia and Hibiscus."

Jazz cracked up as Iris disappeared once again. Iris's grandmother had been a fan of flowers, obviously, but she hadn't gone *that* far. She *had*, however, suggested Iris's name. A lovely one.

Jazz returned to her office. Well, Lily's office, but Jazz had made her own workspace in there with a laptop. Not difficult, considering Lily had a big wraparound desk. Jazz easily fit her own items along one side. As a writer of fantasy novels, she had a portable job, which was why Lily had asked her to stay with Iris.

Her niece was a joy and the climate here in Wyoming, even in springtime, had Miami beat hands down. At least at this time of year.

She surveyed her work area, surrounded by Lily's things. Lily was neat, so that wasn't a problem, but Jazz was much less so. Her only neatness came from the laptop, and a pencil cup that was decorated with a pen that had a colorful flower on the top. A gift from Iris when she'd been eight.

Then, of course, there was her notepad, essential for jotting down everything from ideas to shopping lists. A coaster for her bottle of water or cup of coffee. And the inevitable mess of papers that she'd printed out for one reason or another, and forwarded mail. She didn't even bother to try to straighten up the papers because they had a mind of their own.

She leaned back in the comfy office chair, not really inclined to write, and thought about her niece and her sister.

She'd never visited them here before because Lily and Iris preferred to come to Miami to visit, for beaches, sand and sun, especially during winter months. That was okay by Jazz. She'd never felt any urge to come to the back of beyond.

Now here she was, and she was enjoying it.

Well, she'd finished her day's allotment of writing anyway, so perhaps she should just go to the kitchen to start dinner. Because she rarely cooked just for herself, she was having an adventure with that. She was trying to prepare *real* meals, not just something frozen she could toss in the oven or microwave.

Jazz suspected that Iris would have been happy to survive on hamburgers, but she tried to stick to a training diet for her swimming.

Jazz was all for it, but that meant that a tray of frozen lasagna wasn't a great idea. Anyway, all that swimming created an astonishingly large appetite.

Which left Jazz standing in the kitchen trying to figure it out. Veggies, of course, but Iris also had a need for carbs. Jazz repeatedly felt surprised by the way Iris tucked into them.

Whole wheat and multigrain bread. Usually, but that didn't keep her from eating ordinary rye bread by the ton. Peanut butter was another favorite, but that list wasn't going to turn into a dinner.

Heck, she'd gone grocery shopping after her arrival three days ago and she already realized she hadn't bought enough.

Startling her, there came a knock on the front door. She'd hardly moved three steps when she heard Iris's happy voice.

"Adam! Oh, and you brought Sheba, too."

Sheba? Jazz could hardly imagine. As she rounded the corner into the foyer, she saw a tall, well-muscled man with military-cut light brown hair. He wore jeans, work boots and a khaki work shirt. Accompanying him was a dark red Irish setter whose feathery tail swished the floor happily as she sat.

Iris was already on her knees with her arms wrapped around the dog's neck. "Ooh, you good doggie."

Good doggie returned the hug with a wide grin and repeated laps of her tongue on Iris's face.

"She'll lick you to death," the man said.

Jazz raised her gaze and saw him smiling at her. He was good-looking, too, his face lightly lined from weather.

"Hi," he said. "I'm Adam Ryder. You must be Jazz. And this furry critter is Sheba. Don't ask me why, I still don't know where the name came from. Just popped out of my mouth when I adopted her."

Iris turned her head, still hugging the dog, and said, "Aunt Jazz, I want a puppy."

Jazz shook her head. "And I don't want your mother to kill me." She smiled at Adam. "Come in, if you have time. I'll make some coffee and pour orange juice into Iris."

Man, girl and dog followed her into the kitchen where she started the drip coffee pot. Iris grabbed her own bottle of juice from the fridge. At a quart a day, it wouldn't last long. Iris's appetite amused her.

"I'm sorry I didn't get over sooner to introduce myself," Adam said. "But I was in Cheyenne for a few days. Anyway, I'm your across-the-street neighbor."

Iris planted herself at the small kitchen table, drinking juice from the bottle with one hand while petting Sheba with the other. The dog's tail still swished happily.

When Jazz realized Adam was still politely standing, she said, "Grab a seat. Can I offer you a snack?"

"Unlike this young lady here, I can't afford to snack much. Gone are the youthful days when I could eat any amount."

"I heard," Iris said. "Twenty tacos once, wasn't it?"

Adam chuckled. "I was a string bean with a fast metabolism. After I left the Army, that didn't work anymore."

His smile was engaging, Jazz thought. It lit up his face.

"I still want a puppy, Aunt Jazz."

Jazz looked at her niece. "I'm not doing an end run around your mother. No way. You convince *her*. Besides, who'd take care of it when you're gone all day at school or lost in a swimming pool? Me?"

Iris shrugged. "Walking a dog would be healthy."

Jazz couldn't contain her laughter. "I can walk without a dog."

Iris gave her a sidelong look. "Not as often, though."

Adam spoke to Jazz. "You can't win with this one."

"Apparently not, but I can stand firm."

Iris sighed. "Okay, okay. But I need to get back to my homework. Can I take Sheba?"

Adam answered. "I think she'll follow. She's got kind of a thing for you, Iris."

"Sheba needs a cousin." Iris left the room with the orange juice and the dog at her heels.

Jazz poured the coffee. "Milk? Sugar?"

"Black, please."

Jazz joined him at the table. "Lily mentioned you a couple of times. It's nice to meet you at last."

"Lily mentioned you more than once. Twins are close."

"Sometimes it's like we still share the same umbilical cord. So how about you? Something about you being a carpenter?"

"Handyman. Odd jobs. I like fixing things." His eyes crinkled at the corners as he smiled. "And you're an author?"

"So my fingers and computer claim."

"More than that. Lily showed me a row of your books on her shelf. Must be special."

"First it starts as a hobby. Then it becomes a job. Different feeling altogether."

"I guess I can see that." He sipped his coffee, and silence fell between them.

Small talk between strangers could be awkward, Jazz thought. She sought something to say, then, "How'd you get Sheba?"

"Well…" He drew the word out, teasing the story along. "You see, I was visiting my buddy up north. The guy has a big spread and I like to ride horses. He's always happy to lend me one and send me out into the wide-open spaces."

"Sounds nice."

"It is. Peaceful. Anyway, he has this thing."

"A thing?"

"Yeah. He says he read a veterinary study that said it was better not to fix dogs until they were well over a year old. Something about them being less likely to get overweight. So…"

Jazz chuckled. She guessed what was coming. "Unintended consequences?"

"You could call them that, although Sam didn't seem too upset about it. He's got quite a collection of Irish setters. They're great hunting dogs and pointers. Anyway, a couple of them got together and when I arrived on one visit he had six weaned puppies. The rest, as they say, is history. I've never regretted bringing Sheba home with me."

Then he cocked a brow. "I think I should have come up with an Irish name for her. I keep getting asked about Sheba."

"It's unique."

"Maybe. It seems there is a list of popular dog names with Molly at the top. Bet you Sheba isn't as low as we'd think."

"Do you take her hunting?"

Adam shook his head. "I didn't get her for that. She's a great companion. And I've learned a lot of breed traits from her."

"How so?"

"Well, I never taught her to point, but she does."

"Wow. Really?"

"Yep. And another thing that still floors me. A friend of mine has a parakeet. He was out of his cage one day, flying around and perching on high things, like curtain rods. I'll never understand why Nibbles decided to fly low."

"Nibbles?" Jazz felt her eyes widen.

Adam grinned. "Yeah, because the bird used to bite my friend when it was a baby. So Nibbles."

"Makes sense."

"Anyway, Nibbles got too close to Sheba. Next thing all we can see is feathers sticking out from her jaw. I yelled *drop it* and the dog did."

"Oh my God. I can't imagine!"

"What I couldn't have imagined was that Nibbles was just fine. He shook out his feathers then started squawking at Sheba right in her face. A total scolding."

"How did Sheba take that?"

"She hung her head and took it until the bird flew away."

Jazz thought about it, amused. The image was just too much, but she had to ask, "You're not kidding?"

"I swear I'm not. Bird dog in her, I guess. She never bit down."

"Holy moly."

"That's what I said, only a little more colorfully. That dog is a trip, I can tell you."

"Sounds like it."

Then they fell silent again. Eventually Adam asked, "You haven't been here long yet, but what do you think of our town?"

"So far it's charming."

"It's also small enough to have one hell of a grapevine. As the saying goes, if you don't know what you're doing, ask a neighbor."

"Uh-oh."

Adam shrugged. "It rarely gets nasty, but when people gossip it's bound to happen. I just haven't heard anything like that."

"Thanks for the heads-up. I'll be sure to behave myself."

He laughed. "Always wise, don't you think?"

He rose then, and took his cup to the sink and rinsed it. "I've kept you long enough and I need to get ready for a meeting. If you want anything, I'm right across the street. Or Iris can show you."

Jazz rose, too. "You're fond of Iris."

"Hard not to be. I could say the same for Lily. You got a nice sister. But you got the better name."

He called Sheba when he reached the front door and clipped a leash on her. "Time for a short walk before my meeting. Nice to meet you."

It had been nice to meet him, too. But then Jazz faced the conundrum of dinner again. Maybe she ought to get some cookbooks. No help now, though, when the larder and fridge looked as if a horde of locusts had passed through.

"Hey, Iris," she said, sticking her head into the dining room.

Iris looked up from her laptop. "Writing a term paper," she said. "For physics, if you can imagine." She looked disgusted. "I can see it for English or history, but this?"

"I'd have no idea where to begin."

Iris asked, "What did you need?"

"A grocery list. Or better yet, for you to come shopping with me. I have almost no idea of what your training diet involves, or how much. Man, a quart of orange juice would have lasted me over a week."

Iris looked impish. "You need to walk more. Okay, let's go now."

"But your paper…"

"Can wait. It's not going to get any harder if I come back to it in an hour. Besides, I noticed we're pretty much down to peanut butter sandwiches."

"And I can't even figure out something for dinner."

"The horror! Okay, let's get going."

JAZZ PULLED ON a sweater because she was acclimated to a much warmer client. Iris teased her about it. "This is wonderful weather."

"For those who haven't lived in Florida most of their lives. You're just going to have to deal with me being chilly."

Iris suggested they drive to the store, which gave Jazz an idea of the size of the coming shopping trip. The grocery was fairly busy with people looking for last-minute meal needs, but Iris kept them moving, filling the cart with enough groceries for a football team. As they worked their way along the aisles, greetings were exchanged but there was no time for introductions. Everyone was busy, and Iris didn't slow down enough to talk.

Jazz was astonished by the heap in the cart, but a little more concerned about knowing how to cook everything. Frozen vegetables fine, but some of the fresh ones were unfamiliar to her. A mound of protein bars. Then there was fish, all of it frozen, but it was still a lot.

"I guess I'm going to have to learn to cook fish," Jazz remarked.

"Look it up online. Don't you cook at home?"

"For one? Not often."

Iris just shook her head. "Not healthy, Aunt Jazz."

"So I should crawl under a rock?"

"No," Iris answered pertly. "Just learn. Are you sure I can't get a dog?"

Jazz gave her a humorous frown. "Talk to your mother."

Multiple loaves of whole grain breads, two dozen eggs. Three gallons of milk. Instant grits. How was Iris going to eat all of that?

Well, she must be able to, and she had a perfect figure.

Jazz could have sighed. Her sedentary job made it so much more difficult.

At home, putting everything away proved to be a bit of a challenge. Iris, at least, had a good idea of where things could go. A bit of rearranging in the fridge was necessary, but after a half hour or so everything was put away.

"Now that looks better," Iris announced approvingly with her hands on her hips.

"At least you won't starve to death."

Iris giggled. "The benefit of athletics."

"So…dinner tonight."

"I'll take pity on you."

Jazz cocked an eyebrow. "How?"

"Red beans and rice." She waved a box. "The only hard part is lightly browning the andouille sausage."

"What about your paper?"

Iris shrugged. "It's not due tomorrow, and anyway this doesn't take long."

Nor did it, especially with the rice cooker.

"Now you know how to cook this," Iris said.

"Yeah, and I can buy a dozen boxes now."

Iris laughed. "Check online. Loads of recipes."

"But *I* get to cook."

Iris laughed again. "Thirty minutes. I'll be back for dinner."

Jazz didn't doubt it as she watched Iris head back to her studying.

AFTER THE MEETING with other vets that Adam helped counsel, he took Sheba for her late-night walk. The streets were peaceful, quiet. His favorite time of the day.

He also thought a lot about Jazz. She was definitely Lily's twin, so alike in appearance that it was hard to tell them apart. But Lily had never appealed to him the way Jazz had managed to in just a few minutes. An interesting reaction.

Both sisters were striking, with long inky hair and bright blue eyes. *Black Irish*, Lily had once told him. Iris had the same brilliant blue eyes, but with that tightly curly red hair. Red Irish, he supposed, although the family tree probably wasn't purely Irish. Maybe he'd ask Jazz a bit about that.

Any reason to have another conversation.

He also had plenty to consider after the night's support group. Together, vets talked a lot more than they could with people who'd never walked in their boots. Stories they never could have shared because they were raw, open wounds that others wouldn't understand. Tonight had been especially hard for Winston, a man who'd led his platoon into dangerous places, places where death had stared them in the eyes. They'd done what was demanded of them, but had to live forever after with appalling images, horrifying memories and grief that plagued them almost constantly. Some even hated themselves.

War was an atrocity-making situation, a situation soldiers had to harden themselves against in any way they could. Then they came home. In a couple of days they transferred from war to peace. To a life with different rules and different expectations, and the transition rarely felt like slipping into an old, comfortable shoe. They'd been indelibly changed. Hardly to be wondered that they often had difficulty coping.

Winston had come home to a wife and two young children. Video calls couldn't make up for the loss of shared experiences. He might have taken the family with him to Germany before his deployments but he and Sherri had decided not to uproot the kids that way. In the end it wouldn't have made much difference.

He had come home to a family, especially children, who were virtually strangers to him. The man he had become was a stranger to them.

To top it off, Winston had a truly severe case of PTSD. He'd put up a steel shed in his backyard, then had used it as a bolt hole. For days at a time he wouldn't emerge while he hunkered inside, possessed by his demons. Sherri had left food and drink outside the locked door of the shed, but sometimes he didn't come out long enough to even grab bottled water.

Then Sherri had left him. Now *she* couldn't handle any more and she believed it wasn't good for the kids. In that Winston had agreed with her.

He'd come to this town alone, wandering the back roads, finding secluded places in which to hide when he needed to.

Then he'd parked here, but no one knew for how long. Adam wished for some way to ease the guy's suffering but so far even the meds the VA had prescribed for him made no noticeable difference. Winston was a broken man.

Tonight for the first time, Winston had cut through his reserve and dumped some of his ugly backstory to a group that understood. Winston had wept and raged while he talked, and some of the others had, too, recognizing themselves in Winston's story.

God! Each one of these gatherings evoked a lot in Adam as well. Memories and emotions he kept under steely control but were nevertheless part of him.

Which made him a lousy candidate for feeling an

attraction to Jazz. To any woman. Nope, no innocent deserved to be exposed to his backpack of sor-
rows, hatred, ugliness. Winston was proof of that.

Firm in his decision, he led a happy Sheba back
to the house. That dog was a comfort to him. The
only real comfort he allowed himself.

## Chapter Two

Morning brought bright sunlight and cool temperatures. Before starting her work, after Iris had left for her Saturday training, Jazz set out for that small bakery she'd seen near the sheriff's office. The time shift from Florida had changed her best writing hours, which left her some more time in the morning. She couldn't understand it, but since coming here she didn't at all feel like writing until midafternoon. It should have been the opposite because the time here was two hours earlier.

She figured Iris would be delighted with a bag full of delicious sins and would probably dive into them. As for dinner tonight…well, she was going to have to take stock of the larder and figure out something. Iris had been right about searching recipes online, but it now occurred to her that a list of menus for a week would help her organize the shopping better, with necessary ingredients. At this point she didn't know which items would fit into what recipes and thus she didn't know what to look for. Maybe she ought to try to lay out menus for this week and find out what she still needed.

God, she had a lot to learn. She wondered if Lily had done much cooking, or if Iris's rapacious run through the grocery had simply met *her* desires.

*Sheesh*.

Well, there was the fish. Lots of it. She should start with that.

What mundane thoughts, a far cry from the adventures she wrote. Did any of her characters cook? Hah. Not beyond the requisite pot of something hot, or something easy like beans—her own version of course.

She smiled and nodded at people she passed, all of whom called her Lily. She didn't mind in the least. No point in stopping every time to try to straighten it out or, worse, humiliate people for an understandable mistake.

She just wished she could slip into Lily's shoes in other, more important, ways. Well, she'd only be here for a month or so and developing an inferiority complex wouldn't help much.

At the bakery she met Melinda, a lovely middle-aged woman wearing a white apron and only too ready to show her the contents of her case.

"For Iris?" she asked. "I know what she likes."

"For Iris," Jazz answered with a smile. Last thing she wanted to do was mess this up. She'd have plenty of opportunities to mess up other things.

Ten minutes later she left the bakery with a box

full of treats. A breeze had kicked up and she buttoned her sweater. She just hoped she didn't get used to these cooler temps before she headed back to swelter in Miami.

She left the box of pastries on the kitchen island for Iris, then headed to her computer. The nice thing about this change in time zones was that when her best writing hours rolled around, she'd already had time to do quite a bit of other stuff, like going to the bakery. Except the writing defied her.

Man, this was a whole new way of thinking, not just a new lifestyle. The mundane thoughts that were running around in her brain were unusual for her.

And they'd become boring even to her if she let herself ramble in those weeds for too long.

She put in her earbuds and turned on some moody music that would fit her writing. Music always made it easier for her to write.

JAZZ WAS DEEPLY absorbed in her work when Iris interrupted. "I'm home, Aunt Jazz. Need more time to work?"

Jazz scanned her page and word counts. "I'm almost done for the day. How about I just stop?"

Iris grinned. "What about that pastry box?"

"Oh, that? Some woman wrestled me to the sidewalk this morning and told me to take them for you."

Iris giggled. "Right. Say, can we invite Adam over?"

Jazz blinked. "Sure. I guess. Why?"

"Because he's sitting on his front steps with Sheba and he's not looking very happy. Maybe gloomy."

"You just want Sheba to come over," Jazz teased her. "Okay, round him up. I have enough pastries for an army."

"Better make coffee," Iris said over her shoulder as she hurried away. "From what I've seen, it's essential to life for him."

Jazz closed her document, turned off her music and went to the kitchen to make coffee as ordered.

It must have taken a little effort on Iris's part to persuade Adam to come over because the coffee had finished brewing before she heard Iris return, the click of Sheba's claws on the wood floor and Adam's heavier tread.

One after the other they entered the kitchen, Iris in the lead. "I dangled pastries under Adam's nose," she said. "I think it was Sheba who made up his mind for him, though."

Adam spoke. "I told you that dog would follow you anywhere."

"Only because she has good taste," Iris retorted.

"Hi, Adam," Jazz said when she could get a word in. "Have a seat, and I'm just putting the box of pastry on the table with napkins. Finger food time and no plates for Iris to wash."

"Fine with me," he answered.

Jazz noticed the heaviness in his voice, nothing like yesterday. Iris was right, he was looking gloomy.

Iris brightened the moment. "You hear Aunt Jazz, Adam? She *assumes* I'll do dishes."

Adam half smiled. "I'm surprised she doesn't assume more."

Iris feigned a sigh as she helped ferry coffee and napkins to the table. She even poured coffee for herself. "Better with pastry," she remarked. "Orange juice with this? Blech."

Jazz chuckled. The girl was irrepressible.

"You know," Iris said as she chewed a mouthful of jelly-filled doughnut, "Aunt Jazz isn't correcting anybody when they call her Lily."

Adam looked at Jazz. "Why not?"

"Because it doesn't matter. I'll only be here a few weeks. Anyway, Iris's mom can come home and apologize for *my* mistakes."

That drew giggles from Iris. "I like that." Then she turned her attention to Adam. "Aunt Jazz has the best name of all the girls Grandma named. I mean, think about it. At least Jasmine can be shortened to Jazz. Very cool."

One side of Adam's mouth remained lifted, but the smile didn't reach his eyes. "I agree. Very cool."

What was going on, Jazz wondered. Adam seemed like a very different man than the one she'd originally met. Withdrawn. Iris had been right about him looking moody. His heart wasn't in this little coffee klatch. Sheba sat right beside him, and she looked a bit down, too. God, dogs seemed to have expressions. Maybe more importantly, her tail wasn't happily swishing the floor.

Iris was doing all the bright and cheerful for them, and Jazz felt uncomfortable because she couldn't think of much to say that might lift Adam a bit. But Iris had picked up his mood and dragged him over here. Maybe this would help.

He finished his coffee, without touching the pastries, and looked about ready to leave. Iris forestalled him, jumping up to refill his mug.

She spoke pertly. "You can't leave until you drink that. Anyway, you need to eat a donut or something. Sugar will perk you up and if I eat all of that, I'll get fat."

"Small chance of that," Adam remarked. "How many miles a week do you swim?"

"I don't count the miles, only pool lengths." Iris resumed her seat and reached for a cruller. "These are the best."

Jazz spoke. "Well, that explains why Melinda gave me six of them. She said she knew what you liked."

"She knows me all right."

"And just how, pray tell, do these pastries fit into your healthful diet plan?"

Iris grinned. "Pure ugly calories. Sometimes I need a bunch of them. Just not too often."

A smile finally creased Adam's face. "You mean you need to indulge once in a while."

"Well, that too." She pushed the pastry box toward him. "So do you."

At last he took a cruller. "Saving you from yourself."

Jazz, who'd been picking on her own bit of muffin, was glad to see the interaction between the two of them. She suspected that Iris got further with him than most people.

Jazz decided to stick her toe in the water. "Adam, you said you're a handyman. Does that mean you do everything, or do you limit your skills?"

"I do pretty much everything household. I stay away from cars, though. Not because I can't do them but because I don't want to take any business from Roger's garage. I have enough work anyway. A lot of people are pretty handy themselves, but there are jobs they don't want to do. Like squeeze under a sink to fix the pipe fitting on a dishwasher. Or to actually repair one." He tilted his head. "Dishwasher pumps always get them to call. Washers, dryers, stoves, refrigerators. A little of everything, which I guess was a long answer to your question."

At least he was talking, Jazz thought. "That's a pretty useful skill set. So plumbing? Carpentry?"

"Depends on the job. I install water heaters, faucets. As for carpentry, small jobs."

"He's done some work for Mom," Iris announced.

"But I couldn't fix the washer," Adam reminded her. "When those tubs go out of balance permanently, that's pretty much all she wrote."

"Noisy, too." Iris wrinkled her nose. "I was surprised it didn't fall apart."

"Might as well have."

"So now we have this fancy-schmancy one. I think Mom cringes every time I use it. But she still makes me do my own laundry."

Jazz was startled. "Of course she does! She's not a maid."

"That's what she says." Iris looked mischievous. "Darn, expecting me to keep up with all those towels."

"Trust me," Jazz answered, "I'm not the laundress, either."

Another giggle escaped Iris. "I'm not as bad as I pretend. Mom works. You work. But that doesn't mean I can't try to wriggle out of things."

"Wriggle harder," Adam suggested. "Maybe you can fool your aunt into letting you out of more."

Iris sighed. "I wouldn't like it if Mom heard about it. She's not as nice as you are, Aunt Jazz."

"You only think I'm nice."

After a bit, Iris excused herself, announcing that she still had that paper to finish.

Jazz looked at Adam, and thought he appeared uncomfortable. "Would you rather be somewhere else?" she asked him point-blank.

"I don't mean to be rude." His brown eyes met hers, then slid away. "Sorry, there are times when I'm just not good company."

"We all have those times." But she sensed he

meant something more than an ordinary mood. No way to ask him, however, but she couldn't help feeling bad for him.

"I'd better go," he said, rising and reaching for his cup.

"Leave it. I'll get it."

Then she watched him walk away, a subdued Sheba at his side. What the hell was going on?

## *Chapter Three*

Four more weeks before Lily returned. Jazz was settling into a routine, and she'd learned how to cook fish with several different recipes. Fish was great but she needed something more for herself.

She opted for walking to the grocery. It wasn't that far, the walk would be good for her and besides, the eco awareness in her made driving seem like a sin when it wasn't necessary.

However, she soon noticed something different. Yes, the trees had begun to don cloaks of spring leaves, a beautiful feathery view.

People still greeted her when they passed, still calling her Lily.

But something had changed.

She felt watched. Not casually, as locals might have done, but something more intense. Awareness made her neck tingle.

Man, was she losing her mind? Why would anyone watch her in this pleasant town? She hadn't had a chance to annoy anyone.

But the feeling persisted, and she put it down to the different environment. Maybe she'd just been too busy adjusting to all the newness to notice the sensation before. Or maybe her mind was creating it. Yeah. Why not? Minds did strange things sometimes.

Shrugging it off, she reached the grocery and purchased a few items that Iris, in her drive through there nearly a week ago, had missed. For cooking. Damn, she was cooking, and every night, too. Lily must have done *something* when she was home. Iris sure didn't expect to take part often.

She guessed she was learning some new things about her sister. The high-flying businesswoman cooked.

Hah! She could hardly wait to tease Lily about it.

Every single day, Iris had something going on, whether it was swimming or oboe lessons. Even some after-school tutorials.

The girl was sure driven, and she didn't expect to be carted around. In fact, she kept needling Jazz to do some more walking. Regardless, Iris was too busy to get into trouble, even the ordinary teenage kind.

As she approached the house, she saw Adam sitting on his front steps again, Sheba at his side. She waved, intending not to bother him, but he rose instantly and came toward her.

"Need some help with those groceries?"

She didn't really. Just three paper bags with handles, but she suspected that rejecting his help might be taken the wrong way. "Thanks." She smiled, and let him take two of the bags. Sheba, she noticed, was off leash but glued right to Adam's side.

"She's a well-behaved dog," Jazz remarked to Adam. "I couldn't imagine a dog being so good without a lead."

"She's special, all right. The only time she leaves me is when Iris is bouncing around. I wasn't kidding when I said the two of them have a special relationship."

Once inside the house, she offered him the inevitable coffee, and brewed it while she unloaded the bags. She hoped she was making him feel welcome. She sensed he needed that, though why she couldn't imagine. This town, so friendly, ought to be sitting on his front porch. It never seemed to be. Was he standoffish as a rule?

"Looks like you went with special items in mind," he remarked. He stroked Sheba when she laid her head on his thigh.

"Well, I'm learning to cook," she replied as she put the last item, green onions, in the refrigerator drawer. "That means as I come up with recipes to use the meat and fish, I have to pick up some items. Right now it's all complicated. For me, anyway. Iris barrels through that store and heaps the cart full according to her own tastes, I guess. Then I have to figure out what to do with it."

He snorted. "Easy for her, hard on you."

"That's the way it is, and I'm not going to be here long enough to try to change her habits."

"That might take forever anyway." This time he poured coffee for them both and they sat together at the kitchen table. "Did you know what you were getting into when you agreed to do this?"

"Mostly, I think. Lily and Iris like to visit me in Miami, although I could feel offended and think they come for the beaches." She laughed. "At least twice every winter. That's okay."

"But you've never come up here to visit."

She shook her head, still smiling. "No beaches and no ocean."

That at last drew a genuine smile from him. "Feel like the Hotel Paradise?"

"I know some people who do, but not me. Iris and Lily are easy guests. Besides, they get my nose out of the computer and introduce me to good restaurants."

"So no cooking?"

Jazz laughed again. "No cooking. No extra laundry or cleaning, either."

"Good houseguests." His face grew thoughtful. "Remember how Iris complained her name didn't allow for a cool nickname like yours?"

Jazz nodded. "Interesting thing to notice."

"That young lady has some interesting thoughts in her head. Anyway, I was thinking about a nickname for her, and wondered what you'd think of *Irish*."

Jazz rolled it around in her head for a few moments, then said, "I like it. Her opinion is the one that matters, though."

"Of course, but if you didn't want me to come up

with anything like that, I'd rather know it before I try it. Lily would be okay, too?"

"I'm sure. We're the same head in two bodies, basically. And anyway, the family *is* Irish."

He nodded. "That's what Lily said. All the way back until forever?"

Jazz shook her head. "That's the family story. Mom could prove it at least back to my great-grandmother. Lily hired a genealogist out of curiosity and, sure enough, our first Irish ancestor came over with the British Army during the Revolution. He wound up living in Canada. However..." She drew the word out.

Adam arched his brow. "However?"

"However, as is to be expected of almost any lineage, it's not pure. My sister decided not to show it to Mom when some Welsh and British showed up there. We didn't want to break her heart. But yeah, Irish enough as Lily said."

"I'm a mongrel by comparison."

"I bet you didn't have to grow up with family history being drilled into you."

"No, I didn't. You're right. But Irish is okay?"

"I think so." Jazz shrugged with a faint smile. "See what she thinks, but I'd be surprised if she doesn't like it. Whether she starts using it is something else."

"Might be kinda hard to change her name now."

The gloom started to settle visibly over Adam again. Jazz wondered what she might say to get him to talk about what was bothering him. The best way, she decided, was to confide in him herself. Maybe start the first bridge of trust. Although with only a few weeks, it might be a waste of time.

She smothered a sigh and dove in. "You ever feel like you're being watched?"

He nodded slowly. "Sure, but not for a while."

"You'll think I'm nuts, but I felt that way this morning."

His gaze immediately snapped to her, his face settling into grim lines. "I don't think you're nuts. How bad was it?"

"It made the skin on my neck crawl. I started to get pretty creeped out."

"You would." He nodded thoughtfully. "Did the feeling last for a while?"

"The whole time I was walking to the store. I told myself it was my imagination, but I couldn't totally ignore it. Weird. Anyway, in this town there isn't much to worry about."

"Really? When I was a kid, I remember the old sheriff saying this county was going to hell in a handbasket. Since then we've had some growth, but nothing phenomenal. Anyway, nobody's a hundred percent safe anywhere."

"Oh, thanks!" she said sarcastically. "You just made me feel a whole lot better."

He smiled, a real smile. "I wouldn't give it much thought. We're still a place where almost nobody locks their doors. That sense of being watched might have been nothing. But if it continues, let me know."

"Why? You going to run around looking for someone who's staring at me?"

He flashed a grin. "That's me, fool without a cape. No, I just want to know. I don't like the idea of you feeling creeped out. That's all."

"It won't happen again," she said decisively. "No reason it should. Maybe just a curious person. *Some* people can tell the difference between me and my sister."

"Then they're very observant."

She regarded him curiously. "Can you tell?"

"Just. You have mirrored smiles. When you half smile, the right side of your mouth curves upward. With Lily it's the left side."

She shook her head. "Now that's something I never noticed."

"Why would you? When you look at each other, you're looking into a mirror."

She visualized what he was saying. "You're right!"

"There are probably other things I haven't noticed yet, but I will."

Now his smile was natural and it was good to see. She only wished she dared ask him what haunted him. Then she realized she might not want to know. He didn't appear to be in any hurry to share anyway.

Iris returned very early from school, breezing through the doorway and heading directly for the refrigerator, where she rescued the remaining orange juice. "Hi," she said as she walked through, pausing just long enough to pat Sheba.

"Iris? You're home early."

The girl shrugged one shoulder, the other bearing her backpack. "Teacher education day or something." She flashed a grin. "I think it's actually teacher sanity day."

"It wouldn't surprise me," Jazz admitted. Dang, she loved Iris's view of life.

"Homework," Iris announced.

Jazz stopped her. "Hold on a second. Adam thinks your name has the potential for a cool nickname like mine."

Iris wrinkled her nose. "Nothing as cool as Jazz." Then she asked, "What nickname?"

Adam answered. "Irish."

Iris hooted. "Doesn't that fit, me being red Irish and all. I like it, but nobody will use it."

"Maybe when you get old enough to get tipsy," Adam suggested, which set Iris off into fresh laughter.

"Homework," she announced again, still holding the orange juice. "Then later I've got a training workout at the college. See ya." She headed for the dining room with Sheba on her heels.

"We ought to move to the living room," Jazz suggested.

"Closer to the coffee pot here. Anyway, I've got to get ready for a three o'clock appointment. There's a whistling water heater."

"Whistling? What in the world?"

"Most people never experience it, but there's a pressure relief valve on the top of the heater tank. If the water gets too hot, it starts releasing the pressure. It's a safety mechanism to prevent the thing from blowing up."

"Wow, the things I never knew."

"Most people don't know. Anyway, I need to stock my truck to get ready, and you probably need to get to your own work."

It was true. Since arriving here, she'd begun to have trouble concentrating on her book. That couldn't continue.

"Thanks for the coffee," Adam said, then called to Sheba. He and the dog left quickly.

Jazz stared at the empty space where Adam had been and wondered why she felt so discombobulated. It wasn't just the change of residence. It wasn't taking care of Iris.

It was something more. Some weird kind of unease, and not just because she had felt watched earlier.

She and Lily had often joked that they were psychic, but that usually meant between themselves. This was different.

And it carried a vague sense of doom.

As ADAM WAS loading his truck with water heater parts, hoping something hadn't gone wrong with the heating coil because that was god-awful to fix, he suddenly had the sense of being watched, a feeling he hadn't experienced since his days in the Army.

He looked around, but all he saw was a man parked a few doors down. The guy appeared to be reading a map.

Adam could have chuckled. If the man had wound up on this street and needed a map, he was certainly lost. He was about to go over and ask if he could help when the driver put the map aside and drove off.

Adam went back to loading his truck, but he remembered what Jazz had said earlier about feeling watched. Now he'd felt it, too, but only briefly.

Something must have gotten into the air, he decided. There could be no other explanation for it, not around here.

But he didn't quite believe it.

It was nicer to think about Jazz anyway. She'd managed to drag him out of his morose thoughts, at least temporarily. Much as he tried to avoid these bouts, there wasn't much he could do.

Memories and emotions washed over him like a massive flood, and the gates of the dam only held so long. It was better than it had been a few years ago, but it still overwhelmed him at times.

Not like Winston, though. He didn't think anyone in that support group was as bad off as Winston. But then none of them had rotated through as many tours as he had. Winston had made his twenty years, giving him retirement, but he'd also fought in two wars, Iraq and Afghanistan. Rotation after rotation.

Then he'd come home and his retirement had turned into its own kind of hell. No rest, no peace, no family.

It was a wonder he was still around.

Sometimes Adam wished he wasn't around either. He'd finally found a balance between work that kept him busy enough and the weight room he'd pieced together in his extra bedroom. Working out with those weights caused a rush of endorphins that made him feel much better. Working with his hands helped him to think about other things. The support group, while it freshened some of his mental and emotional scars, gave him a place to vent when he needed one.

And helping his fellow vets in any way gave him a sense of purpose.

Not bad for a guy who'd considered building himself a hermitage in some isolated place, then realized he'd only be reinforcing his sense of isolation.

Because he was different now. Different from most people, and that bridge could never be completely crossed. He was now on a lifelong journey where he'd always feel mostly alone.

Ah, hell. He forced his thoughts away from dark places and turned them instead to Jazz.

Much as the twins might believe they were carbon copies, he was beginning to notice differences, and not minor physical characteristics. Slight differences in outlook, in reactions.

Very slight, probably arising from their different

paths in life. At least discovering those differences was a journey he'd enjoy.

Feeling better he set out to take care of an overheating water heater, one that he hoped only needed a new thermostat.

Now that would add another bright spot to his day.

JAZZ MANAGED TO grind out another five pages in her book. Five pages. She sighed, but it *had* been a grind. Well, it happened sometimes. Waiting for a muse achieved nothing. Muses were unreliable, she thought with a spark of humor. When one arrived to sit on her shoulder, writing carried her away to a place where words and ideas flowed effortlessly.

But more often an editor sat on her shoulder, making her aware of every flaw, every poor word choice, every instance of passive voice. Years of critiques and suggestions had affected her writing. Maybe not all of it good, but she knew her editor would catch it when she screwed up.

How many times had she submitted a manuscript with the feeling she'd screwed up, and with the belief her editor would catch it? A lot of times.

Hah! Most of the time these days she received little criticism, but her confidence still needed some work.

She had just closed her laptop when Lily's landline rang. Lily kept it for business purposes because it was more reliable than a cell for professional calls.

"I hate it when the cell crackles and I miss words," Lily had explained. "Or the famous *I'm losing you* line. I love my cell phone for ordinary calls and texting, but business conversations just don't always make it."

Jazz had noticed that since arriving here. Atmospherics or too few cell towers?

She reached for the phone and heard Lily's welcome voice.

"How's it going, twin?"

"Just fine," Jazz answered. "But I'll never forgive you for putting me in a situation where I have to learn to cook."

Lily's laugh reached across the continents. "It'll do you good. And my peripatetic daughter?"

"Still constantly on the move. I wish I had her energy."

"We used to," Lily reminded her. "When we were her age. Anyway, I figure she's too damn busy to get into any serious trouble."

"That would be my guess. Although how she'd get into much trouble around here beats me."

"Well, there are a few unsavory elements, but not like Miami."

"Yeah," Jazz answered. "I'm still a little uneasy about letting her walk just anywhere, like out to the college."

"You've changed venue. Accept that you need to change perspective, too."

Maybe she was right, Jazz thought. Iris certainly believed she was safe walking everywhere, and Jazz's concern evidently had little to do with here and much to do with where she lived. "How are your conferences and meetings going?" she asked Lily.

"As usual. Much agreement punctuated by even more disagreement about whether, about how, about money. I'm sometimes not sure there's any real agreement at all."

Jazz sighed. "How frustrating."

"I'm used to it. I always bring my mental flak jacket to these meetings. Sometimes I think there are as many opinions in the world as there are people. Or at least cultures. Anyway, we muddle through until we settle on a few things we can do. A step at a time. Or maybe baby steps."

"I don't think I'd have the temperament."

"No," Lily answered frankly. "You've always been the relative introvert between us. You'd rather sit and listen, make your own judgments and keep them to yourself. Me, I'm always getting into it."

"Always to good effect."

Lily laughed again. "Right. Remember Dolly Moore in high school? She wanted to shut my mouth with a good punch."

Jazz smiled, remembering. "She might have, too, except we confused her so much she didn't know *who* she wanted to punch."

"Ah, the good old days. Are you getting mistaken for me?"

"All the time. I let it go. You can make apologies for me when you get back."

Lily hooted. "I'll just blame it on my bad twin. So nobody has figured it out yet?"

"If they have, it's only because they've heard Iris call me Aunt Jazz. And maybe half of *them* are still wondering. Didn't you tell anyone you have a twin?"

"Never seemed to matter. So no one yet for sure?"

"Well, Adam Ryder. He's seen a difference in our smiles. He said the difference wouldn't be apparent to either of us because when we look at each other it's like looking in a mirror."

"Interesting. I never thought about that."

"About Adam," Jazz said hesitantly.

"Yes?"

"I like him, he's nice, but… I don't know. I haven't been here long enough to really judge, but he seems moody."

"That's more of a problem for him than anyone. Army. Afghanistan."

Jazz drew a long breath. "I guess that would explain it."

"Anyway, don't worry about him. Nothing you can do, he has that wonderful dog of his, and he's always great with Iris. He's always struck me as isolated, though, so if he reaches out, just welcome him."

"Absolutely."

Just then Jazz heard the front door open and the unmistakable sounds of Iris's return. She held the phone away from her mouth and called out, "Iris, your mom is on the phone and I really think she'd like to hear your voice. If you can spare a whole minute."

She heard Iris laugh and then the girl appeared. "Oh, all right. I think I can manage." She took the receiver from Jazz's hand.

Jazz left them relative privacy to talk and made her way to the dreaded kitchen. Flounder tonight. She'd never met a flounder that hadn't been on a restaurant plate. Now she was going to get up close and personal.

AN HOUR LATER, after Jazz had unwrapped the now-thawed fish, Iris took the trash out. Another thing the girl never had to be asked to do.

"How'd the swimming go?" she asked over her shoulder as she patted the fish with a paper towel. When Iris didn't answer, she turned around.

Iris stood there, looking confused. She held up a plastic-wrapped bundle of flowers.

"These weren't on the doorstep when I got home, Aunt Jazz. I found them just now. Why would anyone leave dead flowers?"

## Chapter Four

The package of dead flowers lay on the kitchen table. Jazz had told Iris to go take her shower and do her homework, pretending to dismiss the whole thing. Of course, it being Saturday, Iris had no essential homework, and she'd already taken a shower at the pool.

Seeming to understand, however, Iris announced she was going to start her laundry.

But the instant Jazz had seen the dead flowers, for some reason it had clicked with the sense of being watched she'd had earlier.

Her heart still clogged her throat from her initial reaction, and she tried to ignore the way her hands had begun to shake. It had to be a prank. Surely.

But she couldn't escape the sense that it was an ugly message.

She heard the washer start filling, then Iris walked by. "Adam's home. I'm going to visit Sheba."

"Mmm," Jazz answered, the only sound she could make just then. She couldn't take her gaze off those sinister flowers.

Enough, she told herself. Enough. Why get all in a tizzy about something like this? She still needed to make dinner. Flounder. Hell, it would spoil if she didn't cook it somehow.

It also felt like the least important thing just then. Oh, for heaven's sake!

She was just rising from the chair, planning to toss those flowers in the trash bin, when the front door opened. At once she heard Iris accompanied by a dog's clicking claws. That must mean Adam was here as well.

She started to reach for the flowers, to get rid of them before Adam saw them, then stopped. Knowing Iris and her outgoing nature, she'd probably already mentioned them. The three of them walked into the kitchen, Adam saying, "Hey, Jazz."

Iris held up a brilliant yellow tennis ball. "Sheba and I are going to play fetch out back." She and Sheba disappeared out the back door.

Jazz resisted an urge to tell her to stay inside. That would be *so* over-the-top.

Adam looked at the flowers. "Ugly prank. Are you okay?"

"Where I come from this might be a warning rather than a prank. I'm trying not to let it get to me, but it is, a bit."

He nodded. "I read you. I doubt it was intended to be threatening, but I can see why you'd feel differently."

"Dead flowers," she said.

He pulled out a chair and faced her. "Flowers." He repeated the word but it wasn't questioning.

She tore her gaze from the awful gift and looked at him. "I can't help thinking…well…"

"You all have the names of flowers."

She swallowed hard. "Yeah. I've been trying to banish that notion."

He frowned, drumming his fingers. "They look like they come from one of the two groceries and they must be at least a few days old. Nobody would remember who bought them."

"No."

"I'm going to throw them in the trash. I'll be right back."

Even with the flowers gone, she didn't feel much better.

Adam returned quickly but didn't sit with her. "Flounder for dinner?"

"That's the idea. If I can shake this off. If I can remember how I intended to cook it."

"Let me take care of that."

Next thing she knew, he was washing his hands at the sink and looking at the fish. "That's quite a bit."

"Have you ever gone shopping with Iris? Well, if you're going to cook, you ought to stay for dinner."

He flashed a smile that wasn't quite a smile. "Will do. I like to cook sometimes. Better than loading up on cholesterol at Maude's diner, or Mahoney's Bar, or enjoying Hasty's grillmanship at the truck stop diner. Great food but I'm not in the market for an early heart attack."

She relaxed a little and watched him.

He headed for the pantry and soon emerged with a big container of instant potatoes. "Veggies in the freezer?"

"Yes."

"Nothing fancy, but we've got to fill up our athlete."

JAZZ STILL LOOKED DISTRACTED, disturbed. He couldn't blame her. He, too, had made the connection between flowers and that hideous bouquet.

*Dead flowers.* It *did* seem like a message, but that had to be a coincidence. He couldn't imagine anyone in this town, including teens, who would even conceive of such a thing as a prank.

For Jazz's sake, he had to stick to the story that it was all a joke. While it felt threatening, it might not mean anything at all.

In order to make her feel better, he forced himself out of his morose mood and kept up a light patter while he cooked. When Iris came back in, his monologue became a conversation and grew funnier. She jokingly compared Adam to a famous TV cook, and he demanded to know where she was hiding his toque.

And bit by bit Jazz joined in. Exactly what he wanted. She simply *couldn't* worry about those flowers without other cause.

Brussels sprouts, lightly browned in butter, joined a mountain of mashed potatoes seasoned with chicken broth he'd found in the cupboard. Parmesan-encrusted flounder came out of the oven looking perfect.

Adam felt pleased with himself. Yeah, he could cook, but he didn't often and he was glad he hadn't lost his touch. His palate wasn't disappointed either. Both Iris and Jazz appeared to enjoy everything, too, and both complimented him.

Past the flowers, thank God.

He and Jazz finished eating long before Iris, who managed to polish off all the leftovers. Even the mashed potato bowl was cleaned.

"How does your mother afford you?" he asked Iris lightly.

"It's not easy but she loves me."

Adam looked at Jazz. "I can't argue with that."

Jazz smiled. "I'm learning. I never fed a football team before."

"Oh, come on," Iris said. "It's not that bad!"

"Absolutely not," Jazz said swiftly. Clearly, she didn't want Iris to take it to heart.

"You should see what I usually eat," Adam remarked. "Not as much as you, though. Weight lifting."

"That'll do it," Iris agreed. "I told you, Aunt Jazz, you need a dog to walk three times a day."

Jazz laughed. "Great try."

All this time, Sheba had been snoozing quietly near the cabinets, pretty much out of the way. Iris jumped up to take care of the dishes, most of which went into the dishwasher, and Sheba raised her head, wagging her tail.

Adam spoke. "Don't let Sheba talk you into giving her scraps."

Iris giggled. "There aren't any."

"Wonder how that happened," Jazz said dryly.

Adam was glad to see that Jazz had apparently let go of her initial concern about those flowers.

But then Iris did a typical teenage thing. She sat down at the table with a glass of milk and said, "Can you believe those flowers?"

*Thud*, Adam thought as he watched Jazz's face tighten. Crap, he'd been trying to distract her because the last thing he wanted to do was dismiss her feelings.

Nor could he blame her for them. The feeling she had been watched, added to the flowers, added to being in a strange place...well, most people would be disturbed.

He spoke. "Some guy you know probably thought it would be funny." He hoped for a *maybe*. He didn't get it.

Iris drank more milk then used a paper napkin to wipe away the mustache. "Actually no," she replied. "At least I don't think so. But who'd announce it if he was that type?"

"Most likely they fell from someone's trash and someone else did it to tease you."

Iris considered it, then nodded. "Yeah, maybe. An idiotic impulse." Then she rinsed her glass and stuck it in the dishwasher. "A bunch of us are meeting at the church hall to play cards. Gotta run. Back by ten, Aunt Jazz. They throw us out."

She was out the door like a shot, leaving Adam to look across the table at Jazz. Her mood had fallen again.

She spoke. "Would you like to come into the living room? I've got a bad habit from home. I don't have a living room in my studio, so a table serves as the fill-in for everything. But there's no point being stuck in Lily's kitchen."

He'd been about to leave, to give her some space.

But then she said, "I almost didn't let Iris go."

Aww, hell.

Adam made coffee and carried it in a thermal carafe into the living room, along with a couple of mugs.

"What I really want," Jazz said, "is a beer."

"I can run to my place and get a couple of longnecks if you want."

She shook her head. "Thanks, Adam, you've been wonderful this evening. I should apologize for taking up so much of your time. You didn't have to do all this."

"No, I didn't. Returning to civilian life taught me one thing."

"Which is?"

"That there are a few guardrails I have to observe, but the rest?" He shook his head. "I don't have to do a damn thing I don't want to."

That drew a smile from her. "A sense of freedom?"

"Mostly." He sipped his hot coffee, waiting. He was sure she hadn't invited him into the living room because she wanted him to leave.

He knew the room well, with its two overstuffed taupe recliners and matching sofa, a colorful Persian-style rug lying on the floor in the center of the room. Photos of Iris covering the walls which were painted a medium blue. Curtains of a darker blue. And the big-screen TV that once had enthralled Iris and appeared to get little of her attention now. In all, a restful room.

But Jazz didn't look at all restful.

"Talk to me," he said after a few minutes. "You're still upset, aren't you?"

"And feeling like I'm overreacting. Being ridiculous."

"When you figure out how to successfully argue with a feeling, let me know. So, the flowers?"

"Not just them. That feeling of being watched. I *never* feel like that, and now I can't brush it aside. Then this. It's more than ugly. I can't escape the feeling that they were a threat."

She turned her head toward Adam, who occupied the recliner next to hers. Neither of them had raised their feet. "Did Iris say anything else to you about the flowers? Before you came over here?"

A thought struck him, that he'd been looking at this from the wrong direction. "You're more worried about Iris than about yourself."

"Why wouldn't I be?" Jazz shook her head. "Maybe you folks don't think the way I do, but I come from a different environment, unfortunately loaded with threats. Especially to women. I'm not talking about trouble on every street corner, but there's enough of it to make a woman cautious. Here everyone feels safe."

"Mostly," he agreed carefully.

"So I've got a beautiful teenage girl insisting on walking everywhere, even out to the college, often by herself. She's been doing it for years and doesn't see any possibility of danger in it."

"She's probably right," he said firmly.

"*Probably* isn't good enough." Jazz sighed, shaking her head. "Okay, I must be overreacting. As long as she didn't seem disturbed."

"She didn't. Not at all. She just told me it was weird and shrugged."

Jazz eyed him. "But then you came over."

"Well…" He drew the word out. "I guess I just wanted to see for myself."

She smiled lopsidedly. "Do tell."

"I've been in places where I had to be hyper-cautious. I wouldn't consider this town to be one of them, but some old habits die hard."

"Do you still think this was a prank?"

He snorted. "You know high school boys.

They're probably snickering about it, hardly able to wait for Monday to hear Iris talk about it."

Tension let go of her face and shoulders. "Yeah," she murmured. Then she smiled. "When you put it that way…"

Fairly certain that Jazz was okay now, Adam departed with Sheba. He was okay, too. The event had proved to be enough distraction to pull him out of his solitary maunderings over memories he wished he could excise.

But neither of them knew that there *was* a real threat, and the danger lay in wait in the stack of mail on the hall table.

## Chapter Five

Iris had returned home shortly after ten the night before and had collapsed in bed within twenty minutes.

Jazz remembered herself at that age, and how she was apt to stay up late most nights if she could. Iris loved her sleep, understandably, and on Sunday mornings wanted to sleep in.

Jazz enjoyed her coffee with the kitchen window open and birdsong to keep her company. She needed a sweater for this cooler climate but there was something to be said for that. It made her feel snuggly.

Last night's angst had departed, followed this morning by a calmer wait-and-see attitude. Adam's description of teen boys snickering about their prank made sense to her.

As for that feeling of being watched? One day meant nothing. Easy to imagine the whole thing. So she stretched, yawned, sipped more coffee and smiled at the happy bird right outside the window. Spring must feel great to it.

She sometimes wondered how birds handled the winter if they didn't fly south. What did they eat? How did they stay warm? Were there enough bird feeders in the world to keep them healthy? Maybe not, but they were still here.

"Coffee," a rusty voice said.

Jazz turned her attention from the window to see Iris enter the kitchen wearing emerald-green pajamas topped by a white robe that hung open. Her feet had already found their way into some black fuzzy slippers.

"It's there," Jazz answered, amused.

"Yeah," Iris mumbled as she pulled a mug from the cupboard. "I could smell it."

"Did it wake you up?"

"No, some dang bird did. Wouldn't shut up."

"And here I was enjoying it."

Iris glowered as she came to the table. "Not the same bird. Mine is loud. Obnoxious."

"Oh. Say, I was wondering, how do the birds here survive the winter?"

Iris's scowl was fading as she drank coffee. "You should visit some time. The window frames look like they've grown feathers."

A startled laugh escaped Jazz. "What?"

"They hunker around windows where heat escapes, all puffed up like balls. Periodically they attack the bird feeders. I swear Mom puts ten pounds or more of seed in her feeder every week. And they still can fly!"

Jazz giggled. "They sound like you."

"The food maybe, but not that squawking, trust me."

Iris fell silent while she drained her cup. "Okay," she announced, "I've reached first gear. French toast for breakfast? I'll make it."

"Between you and Adam, I'm going to feel like a princess."

"Nah, we both just like good food."

"What? I'm trying!"

Iris grinned. "And I'm kidding. It's a tradition. On Sunday morning, if I want French toast, I make it. Fair trade, especially when Mom can sit back and kibitz."

Jazz poured herself a second coffee. "Does Lily kibitz much?"

"I don't usually give her much reason, but she needs an excuse to be a mother sometimes."

Jazz burst into laughter.

A MAN OUT on the street paused, listening. His face darkened with rage. Laughing? He was going to strike that laughter out of Lily forever. Just as she'd stolen his laughter and his life. And his daughter.

Lily was alone a lot of the time, he'd noticed, which would make his task easier. But he wanted her to feel fear. Terror. All in good time. He'd had plenty of time in prison to stoke his anger and plot.

Only he hadn't plotted for this dinky town. Hadn't ever considered that he'd need to stay out of sight as much as possible. In Miami he could have blended in anywhere.

Conard City was a different matter, requiring a different plan. He had no doubt he'd figure it out and it wouldn't take ten years this time.

But no more laughter for that woman. Never again.

His mind began to roam over the ways he could ratchet up her fear until it turned to terror. There might be *some* advantages to a small town.

He'd liked the touch of the flowers, though. He hoped Lily was already uneasy.

Yeah, she probably was. In some ways Lily was a smart woman. But only some ways. She'd done a lot of stupid things with him, stupid things that meant she had to learn a lesson.

Satisfied about the flowers, he walked on, his mental wheels spinning.

IRIS AND JAZZ spent a fun morning together. Iris regaled her aunt with tales of her amazing victories at cards. Told her about this one boy, named Tony, who kept flirting with her.

"How do you feel about that?" Jazz asked.

Iris shrugged. "Kinda flattered but I'm not interested."

"Is something wrong with him?"

"Not that I know, but where would I fit him in?"

Jazz couldn't repress a grin. "I think that'll change."

"Not without me giving up something else important. Boyfriends can wait until later." She waved an airy hand.

For some reason, Jazz felt Iris wasn't being quite truthful. "I'm sure when you get around to it, you'll have your pick."

Iris screwed up her face. "Everybody's so certain."

"About what, sweetie?"

"That I'll want a boyfriend. Well, he's going to have to fit into my life, that's all I can say. Come on, let's take a walk, see some of the limited sights around here. There are some pretty houses that Mom always admired. A nice park. Ooh, maybe we'll see Edith Jasper."

"Who's she?"

Iris's smile broadened. "A tiny old lady with a very big Great Dane. The sight alone is worth the price of admission."

Jazz had to admit that would be something she'd like to see.

THE PARK WAS only four blocks away, and Jazz was instantly charmed. Kids were running around having fun on the playground equipment or sitting on the grass with cars and trucks. Moms and dads relaxed on benches in conversational knots while keeping an eye out. A few people walked dogs.

Paths rambled around, too, between trees and bushes and even some flowering shrubs. This would be a great place to relax and stretch her legs.

"Why did you never bring me here before?" Jazz asked her niece.

"Because you haven't been here that long, and I've been busy."

"Good point."

"Let's go this way," Iris said, turning them to one of the paths. "I like this one best because of the way it winds around. For some reason it makes me happy."

Amazing, thought Jazz, considering Iris seemed to be naturally happy most of the time.

But the creepy feeling came back as they strolled along the path. Jazz's neck prickled. Someone was staring.

Oh, hell, she told herself. It was a busy park. People all over the place. Any one of them might briefly stare.

*Get a grip, girl.*

They never saw the famed Edith Jasper, however. Iris spied some friends and ran over to them when Jazz told her to go ahead, that she'd just walk home.

She didn't especially want to fall in with a bunch of teen girls who would probably burst with questions about her. But she also didn't want to leave Iris alone.

Damn, she thought. Iris was with friends in a busy park and Jazz needed to get past this senseless uneasiness. She made herself wave, then walked out of the park.

It was a beautiful spring morning and that was exactly the thing she should focus on.

IRIS CAME HOME a couple of hours later. Like a fresh breeze, she wafted into the house and plopped herself at the kitchen table.

Jazz was sitting there with her laptop, trying to work but still finding it hard to concentrate. The different environment seemed to be causing some writer's block. Oh, well, she'd keep trying, and it wasn't as if she was in a time crunch. Yet.

"My friends and I splurged on lunch at Maude's diner. Am I bothering you, Aunt Jazz? Are you trying to write?"

"Trying is the operative word. Success not so much. So how was lunch?" Jazz closed her laptop.

"I loved every mouthful. We had a great time, too. That burger was yummy, but the fries were the best."

Jazz put her chin in her hand. "You actually eat fries?"

"Not often, which makes them better when I do. I am so stuffed now, though."

Jazz smiled. "I didn't know you could get there."

Iris giggled. "Just don't tell my coach about it. But you and I ought to go to Maude's sometime."

"Why is that?"

Iris wiggled her eyebrows. "Because you'd feel your arteries hardening, you'd want to walk more, and since you'd need help with that, you'd get a puppy."

Jazz just shook her head. "Dang, you're persistent."

"I wouldn't be on the swim team if I wasn't."

Jazz couldn't argue with that. "I'm not exactly sedentary."

"No, I see you using Mom's exercise bike. But it would feel so much better outdoors."

Jazz lifted her chin from her hand. "Next time Lily calls, you ask *her* for a dog."

Iris screwed up her face. "I know what she'll say."

"Exactly," Jazz replied feeling momentarily triumphant. Although she privately thought that Iris ought to have her dog. She was a great believer in pets, especially for young people, and if Lily had to bend herself a bit to take care of the animal, she had the benefit of working from home, too.

Besides, given Iris's energy level, she'd probably manage to fit in most of the care herself despite her already packed life.

There was a knock at the front door and Iris jumped up. "I'll bet it's Sheba."

"Sheba knocks?"

Iris's giggle trailed behind her.

It must be Adam, Jazz thought, suddenly wishing she was wearing something better than her frayed jeans and well-worn sweatshirt. And what a strange thought that was. Anyway, Adam was probably still concerned about her reaction yesterday over the flowers. A very considerate man.

The sound of Sheba's claws tapping the wood floor of the hallway proved Iris was right. Jazz almost laughed at the way Iris had believed it was Sheba. Evidently Adam took second place to his dog.

"I'm taking Sheba out back," Iris called as she raced down the hall.

Adam entered the kitchen, and he apparently shared Jazz's thought, saying wryly, "I'm the runner-up."

"That's a fact. Grab a seat. Do you want me to make coffee?"

"I'll make it, if you don't mind. I don't expect to be waited on. I often drop-in. Because of Sheba."

"Iris is really taken with her."

"And I'm willing to share. To a point." Adam moved comfortably around, starting the drip coffee pot, reaching for mugs. "You want some?"

"Please."

Two mugs descended to sit on the counter. These were blue and white, Lily's favorite color scheme. Many of the dishes had a Blue Willow pattern, or something reminiscent of Chinese designs. The motif carried through to the utensil jars which were Delft Blue pottery.

"It looks like you were working," he said as he brought coffee to the table.

"*Trying* to work. Writer's block R us."

"That must be frustrating."

"It will be, if it goes on too long. It seldom does, though."

He nodded. "What do you hear from Lily?"

"Not a whole lot, which isn't surprising. She's told me about these trips. Meetings all day and cocktails and dinner parties in the evening. She must have Iris's energy level."

"But you prefer a quieter life?"

"I'm sort of an introvert," Jazz admitted. "The bigger the group, the quieter I get. And sometimes I just need to find a quiet corner to recharge. I'm not the best guest."

"Friends?"

She smiled. "A small group of very good friends. I'm comfortable with them, and they don't get bent if I go all quiet on them."

He sipped coffee, then asked, "Am I too much, dropping in like this?"

Jazz shook her head. "You're just one person, and I suspect you have a need for quiet sometimes, too."

He arched a brow. "Am I wearing a sign?"

She chuckled. "No. Just a feeling. You're an introvert, as well?"

"I wasn't always." But he didn't explain.

That heightened her curiosity, but there didn't seem to be a good way to ask why. She was always hesitant to pry into people's thoughts and feelings. They'd share what they wanted to, and she gleaned most of her understanding from observation.

They sat quietly for a few minutes. The sound of Iris playing with Sheba drifted in through open windows.

Then Adam asked, "Are you feeling any better today?"

"Pretty much." She bit her lower lip then said, "I had that feeling of being watched again, while we were at the park. It has to be my imagination."

She saw his stare grow piercing. He even stiffened almost invisibly. What the heck?

"Well," she added swiftly, "there are a lot of people in the park."

"True." But he spoke quietly, almost thoughtfully, then drummed his fingers on the table briefly. "That's not a good feeling to have."

"It makes my neck prickle. Which is overkill. I mean, what's there to fear from being stared at? Maybe it's somebody who has the feeling that I'm somehow different from Lily."

"Maybe." He sighed and sipped more coffee. "I'm liking that little scheme you and Iris have hatched about not telling people you're not Lily." One corner of his mouth hitched up.

"It's probably wrong of me."

"Why? It's likely that even if you told them they'd think you were funning them."

"I hadn't thought about that. I just don't want to keep correcting people." She smiled. "I told Iris, and maybe you, that if I messed up anything, Lily could do the apologizing."

He laughed, clearly enjoying the idea. "You'd better mess up something because I want to see Lily's confusion and then her stammered apology."

His response amused Jazz. "I don't think Lily has stammered since third grade."

"What about you?"

"I honestly don't recall. I *must* have been caught flat-footed a time or two. Or more. Or maybe I was just good at wriggling out of things."

Iris returned with Sheba. The dog was panting a bit, but still appeared to be grinning. Iris was, too.

"That was fun," she said, heading for a lower cupboard. She pulled out a large metal bowl and filled it with water, placing it on the floor for the dog. Sheba dove right in.

"It's okay, Aunt Jazz. We keep this bowl just for Sheba."

"Did I say anything?"

"Nope. Ooh, that coffee smells good." She poured herself a mugful and joined them at the table. "Sheba was getting too smart."

"How so?" Adam asked.

"Toward the end, she stopped chasing the tennis ball. She'd just watch it land, then walk over to get it."

"Hah!" said Jazz. "Now that's smart."

"I thought so."

Sheba, done with drinking, sat beside Adam and rested her wet snout on his denim-covered thigh. He began to pet her head, ignoring the dampness. "She's a good girl," he remarked. "But too tired right now to wag her tail."

"Give her a few minutes," Iris said knowledgably. "She's like me. It doesn't take her long to get up and go again."

"Do you ever stop?" Jazz asked.

"Well, I *do* sleep. Sometimes."

ADAM RETURNED TO his house as the afternoon began to wane. Shadows from the mountains had moved in, a false twilight beneath a brilliant sky.

He got the biggest kick out of Iris. She was almost always good for his mood, unless the mood was too black and too deep. On those days, except for his handyman jobs which at least kept him moving, he'd withdraw into his house beyond reach, often working out his dread, anxiety and memories by lifting weights.

Unfortunately, he couldn't bench press anything heavy enough to really work his upper body, not without a spotter. He could have gone to the gym at the college during public hours, but he didn't want to be with so many people. All the noise, the banging and clanging from every direction, could trigger him. Not always, but even occasionally was too much.

Nor was the cost worth it. He'd had to learn to avoid triggers insofar as he knew what they were, and the meds the docs had tried hadn't helped him.

It was what it was, he told himself, the product of his own life choices. He honestly wasn't sure any longer about what had impelled him to join the Army. Not that it mattered. He'd done it and wasn't going to lay the blame for his problems at anyone else's door.

His hip had begun to ache mightily. His limp had grown more pronounced, throwing everything else in his body off balance until he started aching all over. Shaking his head, he gave up the idea of heading for the weights and instead headed for his fridge.

Frozen dinners filled the freezer, except for the ice machine on one side. He pulled out two and headed for that miracle, the microwave.

Except that he'd often thought of it as a time waster. How often did he do nothing else because the damn thing cooked so fast that he didn't have time to do anything else?

When both meals were heated, he carried them into his small living room and placed them on a wooden TV table. First, he popped some ibuprofen and sucked it down with cold beer.

It was going to be that kind of night.

Giving in to reality, he flipped on the big-screen TV to the news. Not that he wanted news. In fact, he mostly hated it, but it was always an easy go-to and prevented him from having to scroll through the guide looking for anything but reality TV. Which wasn't all that real, to his way of thinking. Just a cheap way to fill the slots for advertisers.

Gads, he was turning into a curmudgeon.

He scrolled anyway, because hearing about the latest outrage didn't qualify as distraction. He stumbled on a show about Bigfoot, which might be entertaining. Some myths were fun.

But his thoughts drifted from the show to the women across the street. Those flowers bothered him. Jazz's sensation of being watched bothered him.

He'd felt watched, and the sense could seldom be safely ignored. Although this was a different place than a war zone it shouldn't be dismissed out of hand.

But the combination of the flowers and Jazz feeling watched unsettled him. Worried him. If someone was watching her, why? She hadn't been here long enough to have attracted any real attention.

Then there was Iris. What if the girl was really the one being watched?

His stomach tightened and the meatloaf in front of him lost his interest.

Maybe he was becoming paranoid. Given every other skew in his brain now, maybe he was.

Small comfort. He resumed eating meatloaf that now tasted like ash and trying to watch the pseudo-scientific program that tucked bits of fact in around loads of speculation.

He actually kind of liked the idea of Bigfoot. Imagine a parallel hominid species living a stealthy, concealed life away from one of the world's biggest threats: mankind. Yeah, he could get into that for an hour or so.

The meatloaf regained its flavor, the tension eased out of him.

But he didn't forget. He needed to find some unobtrusive way to keep an eye on Iris and Jazz.

Although watching out for Iris would probably require a whole team, given the way that young woman was always on the move. The thought made him smile faintly.

*Just keep an eye out.*

ANDY ROBBINS KEPT an eye out. He'd been keeping it out all day. Learning your prey's habits was essential to a good hunt.

Now he had to wonder if that big guy from across the street could turn into a problem. He'd spent a lot of time with Lily that afternoon. A lot.

Maybe a romance. The thought ratcheted Andy's anger to a whole new level. Lily was *his*, always had been even when she'd gotten him arrested and convicted. She was *still* his property to do with as he pleased and she needed to pay, not go waltzing off into the sunset with some brooding bear.

He ground his teeth as he stomped through dark backstreets to that lousy motel room. It was hardly better than his prison cell, although even he had to admit that was unfair to the motel and too complimentary to the prison.

He had time, he reminded himself. Time to plan and prepare, and he'd better do both or he wouldn't be successful. Another turn in prison would kill him.

Nor was he a fool. Some might think he was

brainless for getting himself in trouble with the law, but Andy didn't believe that. Betrayal had put him in prison, not his own actions.

If Lily had just behaved like a good wife, none of that would have happened. None of it.

And he was going to get her good.

## Chapter Six

Monday morning brought gray skies and a misty rain. Iris grabbed her usual yogurt and apple for breakfast and an insulated lunchbox she had packed the night before.

She dashed out, calling, "See ya later, Aunt Jazz."

God, that girl was making her feel old, Jazz thought as she drooped sleepily over a cup of coffee. Such an impossible amount of energy.

And now she had the entire day ahead of her to beat herself against a search engine for a manageable recipe that involved a pork roast, or maybe some more fish, or...hey, wasn't there some ham? That ought to be easy. Especially since she seemed to remember seeing a box of instant potatoes au gratin on the pantry shelf. She could manage that.

But Iris wouldn't be home until just before dinner, and Jazz was beginning to feel the misery of her work refusing to budge and the solitude of not being able to meet a friend for lunch.

She guessed she wasn't *that* introverted. She certainly wasn't agoraphobic. Yesterday's walk in the park hadn't been enough outside time.

She yawned, freshened her coffee, then tried to decide her own breakfast. There was enough yogurt in there to feed an entire team, almost all of it mixed with granola. Good enough, although she would have preferred vanilla or blueberry. *Well, heck, girl, next time at the store buy something for yourself instead of being overwhelmed by Iris's needs.*

Then, drowsy or not, she laughed at herself. Iris was overwhelming, yes, but in a good way, and it was only her own customary solitude that kept her flat-footed through this experience.

Well, that and seeming to have lost the anchor of her work. Man, that was something she *seriously* needed to bang her head on. It was one reason she swam in a sea of personal tranquility. Frequent interruptions scattered her thoughts, distracted her from her work, and sometimes made it difficult to pick up the thread.

Writing also fulfilled her in a way nothing else could, even when she started muttering *damnbook* as all one word.

Carrying a notebook, even while away from the computer, had become nearly habitual so if an idea popped up when she was away, she could scribble it down. Lately no ideas had popped up, and her story was lost in limbo.

She ate her yogurt, trying to rattle her brain into some kind of gear. It seemed intent on drifting.

Maybe she ought to just resign herself to this being a vacation, because it appeared it wasn't going to be anything else.

She dumped her waste in the bin and her spoon into the dishwasher. Standing at the kitchen window, she considered opening it, but the mist held her back. Wyoming felt chilly to her Florida blood, and the dampness wouldn't help.

Then she heard the heat kick on. Well, there was a reason for feeling chilly if the heat turned on.

She sighed and headed to the bedroom to dress. Actually starting this day might help.

Jeans and a sweatshirt later, with her black hair caught up in a ponytail, she still didn't feel any more productive. Lost cause.

A brisk walk to the grocery might be in order. Maybe it would clear the fog from her head.

She found one of Lily's light jackets with a hood. It looked warm enough and rainproof, and perfect to cover one of Lily's heavy sweaters. Then she grabbed a couple of the reusable grocery bags and headed out.

The air felt a bit raw, as if winter were moving back in. Surely the wrong time of year? But what would she know?

She didn't encounter many people, but that hardly surprised her. It was a workday, and given the way the air felt, only someone as desperate as she would be out here.

She almost laughed at herself. Desperate? Maybe

so, but not for any good reason. With the hood up, a bulky sweater under the jacket, she felt comfortable enough. Maybe she should borrow more of Lily's clothes. It had been a habit when they were younger and she'd bet her sister wouldn't mind now.

By the time she reached the store, her hands were reconsidering her decision not to hunt up gloves. Once inside, though, she began to warm up. A couple of people said hi, calling her Lily, and she just smiled back, returning the hellos. No one tried to stop for conversation, which was fine with her.

She wasn't quite sure why she was here, except to get out of the house for a stroll. The store made a good destination, and she decided to get some of the fruit yogurt she liked.

Wandering slowly, browsing, she eventually wound up with all she needed to make a large salad for her and the always-ravenous Iris. She even picked up a variety of dressings to pad out the limited selection Lily had.

She also began to have fun. She shopped for herself at home, but this was different, buying larger quantities, choosing items she loved that she felt Iris might love as well. Something different from Iris's choices and the foodstuffs already in the pantry.

Such as fresh broccoli. She made a decent cheese sauce for that. And, look, there were fresh mustard greens to add to her salad. She loved the zing in them.

But given that she had to walk home, she couldn't afford to get carried away.

Feeling better, she stepped out of the store with her two bags and immediately felt those eyes on her again.

This time it went beyond a sense of her scalp prickling to an ice that poured down her spine.

Too much. Too often. Striding along the sidewalk, her pace picked up as she felt as if someone was boring a hole into her back.

She couldn't help but look over her shoulder, but she saw a handful of people. Not one appeared interested in her.

"Hey, lady," a familiar voice called.

She looked to her left and saw Adam in a big white-paneled van. "Hey," she answered, feeling marginally better.

"Let me give you a ride home. I'm headed that way, and it's feeling like it's about to rain."

She was only too glad to accept. He leaned over to throw open the door for her, and she slid in, putting her bags of groceries on the floorboards. He bent and lifted them by their handles, raising them over the seat to place them in back.

"I just finished a job," he said by way of explanation. "Did Iris eat you out of house and home?"

She managed a small laugh. "No, but nearly everything there is her choice. I decided I wanted a few of my own."

"Great idea. You count, too. You were walking kind of fast. Worried about rain?"

"I won't melt. No, I just had that feeling again."

He was silent as he pulled up in front of the house. "How bad?" he asked.

"I felt as if something was boring into my back."

"Damn."

"You think my imagination is running wild."

"Far from it."

The rain started, lightly. A perfectly dismal day, she thought.

"Let me help you get the groceries inside."

"I can do it," she said stoutly.

"Jazz."

It was all he said, so she let him get the bags as she climbed out. When they reached the front door, she saw it. A cry escaped her. "My God!"

"Step over it. Get inside *now*."

She didn't argue, the sight of the gutted squirrel was more than she could stand. He passed the bags to her, then closed the door firmly.

What he did she had no idea as she stood there shaking. A few minutes later, he entered, closing the door behind him.

"Let's get these into the kitchen," he said, taking the bags from her.

She followed, hoping the vision would fade away. It didn't, especially when he grabbed a bucket from the small mudroom and filled it with water from the sink. She heard the front door open and close again.

In a chair, she wrapped her arms around herself and began rocking. This was no joke. It was a threat. She could barely grasp that anyone would do something so cruel. She couldn't believe it was just a nauseating prank. No way.

Adam returned, taking the bucket to the mud porch before returning to sit across from her. "It's gone," he said flatly.

Her response was a whisper. "Thank you."

An eternity seemed to pass until Adam broke the silence.

"This was no joke," he said his voice threaded with steel.

"No," she agreed, her voice still near a whisper.

"I know there's an extra bedroom upstairs across from Iris's. I'm moving in."

Jazz's world reeled. He thought they needed protection.

ADAM WATCHED HER eyes close. She gripped the edge of the table, but there wasn't a damn thing he could do about her reaction. He simply waited while his mind ranged over possibilities. The only comfort he could find was that this clearly couldn't have been directed at Iris.

No, it was directed at Lily, because hardly a damn soul knew she was Jazz.

But what could Lily have done? As far as he knew she was well-liked in this town. She certainly couldn't have done a thing to draw this kind of threat.

"Iris," Jazz said. "Oh my God, Iris."

"It wasn't directed at her."

"How can you be sure?" Her eyes had darkened with fright.

"Because it was done while you were out shopping. If it had been intended for your niece, it would have been there when she came home from school or swimming."

Jazz nodded jerkily. "But I haven't been here long, and no one knows…" Her voice trailed off. Then, "Lily."

"That would be my guess."

"But Adam, you've lived here for years. You'd know if someone had a grudge."

"Well, I don't." He drummed his fingers on the table. "You look cold. You need something hot. Soup? Coffee? Something else?"

"I don't know if I could stomach anything just now." Shrugging, she tugged off the jacket. "Maybe if I let people know who I am?"

He shook his head, his expression grim. "If you do that, it'll just push the threat down the road. Lily will face it when she gets home, and we have absolutely no idea what's going on. Maybe we can figure it out first."

"What if we can't?"

"Then I'll shout from the rooftops that you're Lily's twin and we'll deal with it then."

She nodded slowly. "I wouldn't want anything to happen to my sister." She appeared to be losing some of her tension. "What about the police? I guess I should call them."

Adam noted that she didn't seem to be worried about herself, at least not as much as Iris and Lily. Interesting. They'd been the first of her concerns.

"That would probably be a good idea. They at least need to be aware, but I don't think they'll be able to do anything yet."

"Probably not. How do you trace some dead flowers and a dead squirrel?" She shuddered. "Maybe some coffee. Soup sounds too heavy."

He was happy to oblige, glad to have anything to do that might give her even a smidgeon of comfort. A deep anger was growing in him. What kind of creep would do this?

Combined with Jazz's feeling that she was being watched, he couldn't begin to minimize any of it. Not even to make her feel better. They were past that.

When she didn't reach for the phone, he did, getting straight through to dispatch. Velma's familiar croaky voice answered him. Sometimes he thought that woman was going to die at the console.

"Velma, this is Adam Ryder. I'm at Lily Robbins's house and we've got a problem with a threat. Can you send someone over when you have a chance? No rush."

When he hung up, he poured coffee for them both. Jazz rested her elbow on the table and cupped her chin in her hand.

"This is unreal, Adam."

"Couldn't agree more."

She sighed, and eventually raised the mug to her lips. "I don't know what you do, but this coffee is better than what I make."

"Probably because you don't have to make it yourself."

"Maybe." But her face still didn't have much color. He wondered how to get some food in her. A shock like she'd just had was difficult for the body to handle.

"I'm still worried about Iris, Adam. She's out there so much on her own. Maybe I should drive her."

He understood, but in his gut he felt that was a step too far. The evidence, little as it was, didn't point to the girl. "She's rarely alone, Jazz. And you can't coop her up here like an unhappy bird. She'd hate it, probably never forgive you, and be trying to find ways to escape."

She nodded and sighed. "I'm here only because she didn't want to give up everything to go with Lily to Europe. Imagine that."

Adam managed a rusty laugh. "Your niece has been a world traveler for years. Any one of her friends might leap at a chance to go to Europe, but not Iris. She's been there, done that."

At least that drew a faint smile from Jazz. "True."

"Now let me put the groceries away. You supervise."

"I'd forgotten all about them!"

"Hardly surprising." He rose and began to empty

bags, spreading the contents on the counter. "I'm reasonably sure the yogurt goes in the fridge. After that it may be a foray."

"I'm not sure where Lily keeps everything."

Adam glanced over his shoulder. "Organize it for *yourself.* Lily didn't leave you a map so she'll have to deal with it when she gets back."

Jazz snorted. "My sister has never been big on organization except in her job. She might never notice."

The threat hadn't vanished but Jazz's fear had settled down. Adam felt relief. "I don't know when Jake Madison is going to get here," he offered as he put the last item away. "I'll run over to my place and get what I need for a few days. If I see the black-and-white out front, I'll hurry back."

She looked at him, her jaw dropping a bit. "You were serious about staying with us?"

"Hell, yeah. Get used to it."

JAZZ WAS MORE grateful than she would have believed. Honestly, she was now afraid of being alone. She couldn't forget the sense of eyes being on her, either. The two things felt inextricably linked now.

Someone *was* stalking her.

Worse, despite Adam's reassurance, she was more worried about Iris. In Miami she'd never let a girl Iris's age run about so much with so little supervision. Hell, it wasn't any safer for a grown woman. Places you didn't go, neighborhoods you avoided. Oh, a whole laundry list of things. A subtle form of repression, she supposed, but staying safe was paramount.

Here was different. Clearly. She didn't believe her sister would have allowed this much freedom if she didn't believe it was safe.

But Jazz remained uneasy. On the one hand, she wanted to protect Iris. On the other, she didn't want to frighten her niece. Rock meet hard place, she thought.

Wait and see appeared to be the only approach.

The police chief arrived just as Adam was carrying a large duffel bag across the street. Jazz opened the front door to greet both men, the sight of Adam so welcome she nearly sagged.

*Chicken.* No reason to be terrified of being alone. Not yet.

The cop greeted her, extending his hand. "Howdy, Ms. Robbins. I'm Jake Madison, chief of police. I hear you had a little problem today?"

Jazz stepped back, opening the door wide. "Please come in, Chief. Oh, and you, too, Adam." Sheba, as always, was on Adam's heels.

Adam dropped his bag with a thud near the hall table.

Jazz led the way into the living room, and once everyone was seated the chief asked, "What happened?"

"First I need to explain something," Jazz said. "I'm not Lily Robbins. I'm her twin, Jasmine Nelson."

Madison nodded. "I'd never have guessed it."

"It's not obvious," Adam agreed.

"Anyway," Jazz continued, "I haven't been making a point of it. I'll only be here a few weeks and there's no reason to leave everyone scratching their heads about who is who."

"I can see that. Okay, so you're not Lily. Does that fit somehow with the threat?"

"It might," Jazz began. "The first thing was a bouquet of dead flowers on the porch. Iris found them."

Madison arched a brow. "Dead?"

"Very. All I could think was that it was intentional. I didn't want to, but with Iris, Lily and me, Jasmine…well, I couldn't quite shake it."

Chief Madison nodded. "I can see why."

"I had just started to believe it was a prank of some kind, but then today…" Jazz hesitated, her mind jumping back to what she'd seen with her stomach turning into a hollow pit.

She blurted it out. "There was a gutted squirrel on the front porch, right outside the door."

"Hell," said Madison. "Where is it?"

Adam spoke. "I put it in the trash, but you can see it if you want. I also washed the blood off the porch."

"Blood?" Both of the chief's eyebrows lifted.

"Blood," Adam repeated. "Enough of it."

Madison shook his head, his lower jaw thrusting forward as his lips compressed. "It was done out there."

"It had to have been."

Everything inside Jazz curdled and turned cold. Her voice dropped to a ragged whisper. "That was done *on* the porch? But how? Wouldn't someone have seen it?"

"On a morning like this?" Madison shook his head. "Wouldn't take long, either."

Jazz covered her mouth with her hand, a new wave of shock ripping through her.

"Doesn't sound good to me," Madison said. "But right now, without evidence of a useful kind, I don't see what we can do except keep a close eye out. And we'll do that, Ms. Nelson. Around here we're not so busy we can't look after a neighbor."

He rose, then offered something more. "We can ask around discreetly. See if anyone might have noticed anything. We'll let you know. Adam? Can you show me that squirrel?"

Jazz didn't feel a whole lot better as the two men went outside. On the front porch? Someone had done it right there while she was at the store?

Horror began to creep in with fear.

ANDY ROBBINS WAS fairly pleased with the result of his little present. So she'd gotten unnerved enough this time to call the cops. Victory for him.

He wanted her fear. Eventually he wanted to smell it, to taste it, to see it on her face and in her eyes. But that had to wait. Later, he'd enjoy every minute of his revenge.

For now he had to be content to watch it unfold bit by bit.

Maybe it was getting time to ratchet up even more.

Smiling he wandered down the street after his obligatory gawk at the cop car. Had to act like everyone else.

Which was harder than he would have supposed after prison. Seeing the cop just made him want to run.

## Chapter Seven

Iris appeared surprised to see Adam when she arrived home with her instrument case in her hand and a heavy backpack hanging from the other shoulder.

"Hey, what's up," she asked before dumping her load. "I'm not used to seeing Adam here making dinner."

"Get used to it," Adam answered. "I'm moving into the spare bedroom for a few days."

Iris's eyes widened. "How come?"

"I'm waiting for an exterminator. Whenever he gets done, Sheba and I won't be able to go back until the fumes dissipate."

Iris's eyes widened, then she giggled. "Adam has bugs!"

"It happens to the best of us."

Still grinning, Iris headed toward the dining room, followed by Sheba who had been quietly snoozing near the back door.

"Great save," Jazz said quietly. She'd been wondering how she was going to explain this.

"I hate lying, but sometimes it's necessary." He was working on some kind of casserole that was consuming diced chicken breasts, green beans and cream of chicken soup to which he'd added a half cup of white wine. Jazz had offered to help but he had reminded her of the old saying *too many cooks spoil the stew.* "You'll love this. One of my favorites from childhood."

"Did you *have* a childhood?" She meant to tease him but got a serious answer.

"Not one I care to talk about. According to Lily, yours was pretty good."

She felt bad for touching on something Adam apparently found painful After a moment, she answered him. "We were very lucky. Since growing up, I've learned just how lucky. Good parents are hard to come by but Grandma kept everyone in line."

He smiled over his shoulder. "Was there much keeping in line?"

"Well, as Grandma used to say, age had taught her patience with children. Of course, she wasn't raising us and trying to make us good little kids. She was willing to let us cut loose."

"Then Mom and Dad had to cope with the results?"

"There didn't seem to be many bad results. But

how many parents would allow a kid to use an entire roll of clear tape on open boxes?"

"Not many, I'd think."

At last he popped the casserole in the preheated oven and set the timer. Then he surprised her by pouring her a glass of the Chardonnay he'd just used.

"Medicinal." He winked.

It was a great Chardonnay, a table wine. "You didn't use a cooking wine?"

"Rule—never cook with a wine you wouldn't drink."

He joined her at the table with some of the coffee he'd made just before he started dinner.

"How are you doing?" he asked seriously.

"Better. Over the shock. Just getting angry now."

"I'm not surprised. The worst part is wondering who is that cruel. Or maybe that Iris had been meant to find it."

"God, what a thought! You've been trying to tell me this isn't directed at Iris."

"Yeah." He sipped from his mug. "I'm inclined to think it wasn't. She always comes home late, and you *do* go out, like this morning. You may be an introvert, but you're not a hermit."

She nodded, tasting the wine again. "Then why?"

"If we knew that, we'd be half the way toward solving the mystery."

It was true, but the question kept bothering her. Why? *Why?*

Iris surprised them by clearing off half the dining room table and setting it with Lily's Blue Willow china. The casserole, served over egg noodles, tasted as good as Adam had promised. Sheba lay patiently at Adam's side.

"Does she need some exercise?" Iris asked about the dog.

"Always."

"Then I'll take her out back after supper." She wrinkled her nose. "No dessert?"

Adam lifted a brow. "I think you can read the directions on the brownie mix."

Iris laughed. "Caught."

"Homework?" Jazz gently reminded her, taking a stab at being a responsible adult.

"Not much tonight. Later this week it might get heavy. I'll take Sheba out now, and get the dishes when I come back in. You two ancients relax in the living room."

"The mouth on you!"

That drew more laughter from Iris. Sheba followed her instantly when Iris picked up the tennis ball from the foyer.

"It's miserable out there," Jazz remarked.

Adam shrugged. "At least we don't have to be out in it."

They moved into the living room, and this time Adam poured them both a glass of wine.

"I wouldn't have taken you for the wine type," Jazz remarked.

"Oh, I have a broad range of tastes. The bottle of beer you think I should be holding is in my fridge."

Jazz's spirits had begun to rise in part, she was sure, because of a delicious hot meal. And Iris would lift anyone's mood.

"I feel like I was such a chicken today."

Adam shook his head. "No, you weren't. That was a shocking discovery. It appeared threatening."

"Appeared?" She didn't know if she liked that word. It *had* been threatening. There was no other way to see it.

A few seconds passed before Adam spoke. "I wasn't dismissing it. Not at all. But right now all we have is the *appearance* of a threat."

"But the flowers!"

His expression grew grim. "Believe me, I haven't forgotten."

Jazz sighed, trying to shake the gloomy feelings and get back into the better mood she'd begun to develop at dinner. "I'm being a drag."

He put his wineglass on the side table and leaned forward, resting his elbows on his knees as he looked at her. "Sometimes the brain takes a while to process things. It keeps running them over and over until, hopefully, it's done with them."

She studied him, sensing a deeper meaning in his words. "You have experience with it?"

He grimaced. "War."

One word, and it shook her. She forgot everything else except a blooming ache for him. "Still?" she asked quietly.

"Yes."

Oh my God, she thought, unable to express the emotions that overwhelmed her. *Oh my God.* She couldn't think of a thing to say that wouldn't sound trite or maybe stupid.

He spoke again. "Everything in life has a price. Some worse than others."

"That's awfully philosophical!" She could scarcely believe he could toss off those words. The ache in her heart grew stronger. "How bad?"

"I learned to manage. Various activities."

*Manage.* That meant he was still dealing with all those memories. Now she felt small for freaking out over dead flowers and a mutilated squirrel. Yes, they were bad, even frightening, but nothing to compare to his life then and now.

Small as she felt, she didn't say anything about it. He'd only try to reassure her that her reaction was normal. Maybe it was. But for the first time she wondered how the sight of that squirrel had affected *Adam.*

He'd seemed so calm, so in charge. God knew what kind of gut-churning reaction it might have caused in him.

He hadn't dismissed her shock or fear. Instead he'd taken charge again, moving into the spare bedroom. Mostly to make her feel safe, she guessed.

"You don't have to stay here," she said presently.

"Trying to get rid of me?"

"No. Oh, no! It's just that you have other things to do than ease my fears." Her probably exaggerated fears.

"No, I don't. Anyway, I have bugs and I still need a bed to sleep in."

At last he drew a laugh from her. She couldn't help it. "That was brilliant."

He flashed a smile. "I have my moments."

Iris returned, both she and the dog shedding water. "Sheba needs a rubdown," she announced. The weather had done its usual on her stubborn hair. It frizzed every which way. "Don't worry about towels, Aunt Jazz. Mom keeps a stack of microfiber towels for cleaning and for Sheba. Doesn't she, girl?"

Sheba appeared to grin.

"Come on, Sheba, into the kitchen with you before you decide to shake off any more water."

"It appears Sheba is a welcome guest here," Jazz remarked to Adam.

"As if Lily has any choice, given Iris's attachment."

"She wouldn't object. I know my sister."

"Besides, it probably calms Iris's pining for her own dog."

He had a point, Jazz thought. Then she realized that her earlier fear had given way to her appreciation of the handsome man who sat across from her. God, he was attractive.

Oh, not that. Please. She'd be leaving. He had his own life. He could become a complication she didn't want and a complication he probably didn't want for himself. And just for sex? Because that was all there could be.

She rose, needing to get control of all her runaway feelings. "I'm really tired. I'll see you in the morning." Not a single qualm about leaving him alone with Iris. She trusted him completely, she realized.

Oh, man, that was bad. Very bad.

He spoke. "I think I will, too, once I've stolen my dog back. Sleep well."

That didn't happen because she couldn't stop thinking about Adam in the room right above her head. Every time he took a step or two, she heard the floorboards creak.

What was going on? Was her brain playing games to distract her from the squirrel?

Yeah, she decided. That had to be it. No other reason.

ADAM WASN'T DOING much better at the whole sleep thing. He paced for a while in the small room, then realized he was probably disturbing Jazz. He sat on the edge of the single bed, listening to the springs creak.

That squirrel had stirred him up again. A small wedge that opened a door to bigger, grislier memories. Hell. He didn't want to wrestle with his demons tonight. Not tonight. They'd mostly given him a break for the last week or so, a time of peace he cherished.

But all it took was one trigger. Today had come close to triggering him. He'd managed to clamp the lid on it, but now the slime was trying to seep into the open.

He swore quietly. Sheba immediately jumped up onto the bed and laid her head on his thigh. He stroked her gently, grateful for her love and doggie kindness. Always there, always ready to let him know she cared. A companion who never abandoned him.

"You're the best girl, Sheba."

She nosed him in response.

There had been times when he hadn't been sure he'd make it except for her. Times when she'd been his lifeline, his last tether to the present.

The slime seeped away little by little, driven out by Sheba, by thoughts of the woman sleeping downstairs. It was odd, but he'd never felt this way about Lily.

At last he felt the touch of amusement. Yeah, it had plenty to do with something else about Jazz although he couldn't identify it.

But he was worried, more worried than he wanted to let on. Yeah, he'd called Jake Madison to come over, but that still hadn't told her how seriously concerned *he* was.

There was nothing random about what was going

on. Jazz suspected it, but Adam knew it in his gut. Gut feelings had saved his life more than once and he never ignored them.

He had one now, and it was strong. He guessed that exterminator was going to have to take a while getting here, because he wasn't moving back to his place until he was sure this was over, or they found the creep. If this was supposed to be humorous, someone needed a shrink. If it wasn't, well the guy was still a sickening creep.

The worst was that creeps like that were too often unpredictable.

## Chapter Eight

The morning dawned gray, promising another wet, drizzly day.

"We're usually dryer than this," Adam remarked.

Iris looked up from her oatmeal. "Climate change," she announced.

"Not global warming?"

Iris shook her head. "Climate change. The weather is all over the map."

Adam looked at Jazz who was smiling. She spoke. "She's right. I live in Miami and I'm closer to it. We're flooding more than ever, and hurricanes are growing stronger."

"Yup," said Iris. "And coming closer together." She jumped up, rinsed her bowl and spoon in the sink and put them in the dishwasher. Then she grabbed her backpack and headed for the front door. "I might be home early tonight."

"Why?" Jazz asked.

"Some of the swim team are sick. We may call off practice." Her voice trailed after her. "Bye!"

"Dang," Jazz said. "That girl is something else."

"Smart, too," Adam replied. "Global warming isn't a popular subject in these parts."

Jazz gave him a wry look. "Climate change," she reminded him. "And I'm not surprised. Few people want to think about it, let alone talk about it. It's too big to get a handle on."

"Understandably."

Jazz noticed that he didn't offer an opinion one way or another. Did he agree or disagree?

"Listen," he said, "if I don't take Sheba for her morning walk, she's going to bust. Come with us?"

Jazz hesitated, but only momentarily. Despite the chilly wet day, a walk sounded good. "I'd like that. Let me grab some warmer clothes."

"Do you have any?" he joked.

"Well…" Then she shrugged. "When I was in an urgent care office a few years ago, we were having a fifty-degree morning. There were four people chatting, and one of them said the office had told him to come early because the cold would keep a lot of people away until it warmed up some."

Adam nodded, encouraging her to continue.

"That's when I got a bit annoyed because he thought it was *funny* that anyone would think the weather was cold. He was laughing about it. And I'm sitting there thinking, *Damn Yankee, you try living down here full-time for a few years and you'll have a different idea of cold.*"

Adam laughed. "I didn't mean to be insulting, but *do* you have something warm to wear?"

"Lily has plenty. I'll find something."

"And I agree it's cold out there. Thirty-six degrees and drizzling. Nobody would be warm."

It was her turn to laugh as she hurried back to the bedroom. Adam was good company, she decided as she pawed through Lily's drawers and closet. She found a pair of blue wool pants and a thick sweater. Thirty-six degrees? Deeper in the closet she discovered a warm jacket that appeared to be waterproof. It even had a hood.

"Success!" she announced as she returned to the kitchen.

"You look ready," he agreed. He pulled on his own jacket, clipped a leash to the now-dancing Sheba, and they headed out. The only difference this time was that Jazz made sure she'd locked the door. Not that it would prevent another ugly present on the doorstep.

But she didn't want to think about that. The world smelled fresh, maybe because of the drizzle. She pulled up her hood and enjoyed watching Sheba explore her world. Judging by the amount of time she spent running her nose through grass that had barely started to green, everything must have changed for her overnight. She certainly seemed to be absorbed.

In between sniffs, Sheba pranced.

"That dog has the right idea," Jazz remarked.

"What do you mean?"

"She's loving life. Very much in the moment."

"Yeah," he answered. "Humans spend too much time living in *tomorrow*."

"I never thought about it that way, but you're right. Planning ahead. Even worrying ahead."

"Exactly. The worrying ahead is the part that perplexes me. Half the things we worry about, at least half the things, never happen anyway."

"Then there's that proverbial bus. How do we even know we'll be here tomorrow?"

"Sometimes we don't."

A bit of her joy in the morning dissipated. *War.* He would certainly know that tomorrow might never come. Or even the next hour. She wondered how much of that lingered with him but felt she didn't have the right to ask.

In some ways, Adam struck her as a very private man. She supposed that was okay with her as she was running out of words anyway. An interesting comment for a writer to make, she thought wryly. Although lately she seemed to have run out of words for the page as well.

When Sheba had filled her nose, done her business and pranced for a while, she was the one who tugged the leash in the direction of home.

"She must be getting pretty cold," Adam remarked. "I'm surprised she didn't want to go back sooner."

Jazz, with her hands freezing even in her pockets, couldn't have agreed more with Sheba. "Maybe she was having too much fun to notice."

But maybe not only the dog. Jazz's nose felt nearly frozen, and her cheeks weren't doing much better, but she'd been having a good time walking anyway. This was evidently the Wyoming version of a Florida walk in the heat and humidity.

When they got home, Sheba started running throughout the house as fast as she could.

"The zoomies," Adam remarked. "As soon as she slows down, I'll towel her off. I think she's warming herself up, though."

"Wouldn't surprise me." Jazz hung her sister's jacket over the back of a kitchen chair to dry it off. The wool pants, however, kept her warm. She headed for the counter to brew some fresh coffee. Warm. Hot. She needed it now.

At least there had been no surprises at the door.

She was still troubled about why anyone would do such a thing, but troubled or not she also knew there was no answer. Human behavior often couldn't be explained, especially when it was outside the norm.

Sheba apparently loved being rubbed down, and Jazz smiled as she watched the dog grin and wiggle herself until she got toweled in the places she wanted.

Adam disappeared around the corner with a handful of small towels, then returned. "I laid them over the washer and dryer to dry out."

"Thanks."

The coffee was ready and he didn't wait for Jazz to hop up and serve it. He poured two mugs and brought them to the kitchen table.

"Okay," he said. "It was raw out there."

"Just a bit. I think my cheeks might be raw, too."

"They're certainly red, but I imagine mine are, too. Looks like a winter sunburn."

"Hah! Good one."

He glanced toward the kitchen window. "It's not getting any better. Two days of this crud. Misty, wet, cold. Tomorrow doesn't promise to be any better."

Then he lifted one corner of his mouth. "Discussing the weather. How boring. The kind of thing strangers and ranchers do."

"We *are* kind of strangers."

That widened his smile a bit. "I may be a relative stranger to you, but I don't feel like you're one to me. I've known Lily since she moved here, and we've talked a lot, including about you. No, I'm not getting confused by the similarity in appearance."

She believed him since he'd picked out a difference right from the beginning. "I hope she didn't tell you everything."

"I'm sure she didn't. Would you tell on her?"

"Never."

"See?" He shrugged slightly.

Jazz, not gregarious by nature, wondered what else she could say. He'd already made it clear that he didn't want to talk about his childhood, and she was sure Lily had hit all the high places in theirs.

In the silence, she heard the heat kick on again. About time.

"Listen," he said presently, "you need to work. I feel like I'm stealing your time, and Iris will be home early. Grab an apple or something and get to it. I've got some books to read."

Well, she could hardly argue with that. "Thanks." She left her coffee mug and went to the office. High time she put some words on her computer screen. Well past time. Maybe she'd write a man like Adam into her book. Just similar, because she didn't use real people in her novels. That would be a violation of trust. But loosely modeled? Very loosely modeled.

She felt good sitting down at her laptop for a change. Since arriving here it had looked too much like a chore.

Maybe her brain wasn't dead after all.

JAZZ HEARD IRIS come in early. She was immediately disturbed because her niece's stride was slow. She shut her laptop and hurried out to the hall in time to see Iris toss the mail on the hall table and drop her backpack. No smile from the girl, just a dragging step.

"Iris? What's wrong?"

"I think I caught the bug that hit the swim team. I don't feel good, Aunt Jazz."

Sheba came running from somewhere else in the house as she always did when Iris came home, but this time she drew up short, watching. Maybe she sensed something was wrong?

"You don't look good." Jazz crossed to her and laid a hand on Iris's forehead. "You feel warm, too. Go make yourself comfortable in the living room and I'll bring you some chicken soup. If that sounds good, anyway. And maybe the thermometer, if I can find it."

"The soup sounds good." Iris managed a tired smile. "I don't know where the thermometer is. Mom hasn't used it since I was in elementary school."

"Need a blanket?"

"I dunno yet."

Jazz immediately tried to help the girl out of her jacket, but Iris shrugged her hands away. "I'm not helpless. I just don't feel good. Sheesh, you don't have to hover."

Jazz didn't take offense. How could she? Besides, she'd never liked being hovered over herself. "I'll just get that soup."

There were only a couple of cans in the pantry, but she remembered a whole chicken in the freezer. Surely she could remember how to make homemade chicken soup. Well, and roast the darn thing as well. The chicken meat made a good meal, and the broth made from the carcass was wonderful.

She glanced at the clock and figured she didn't have enough time to get it ready for that night. Maybe tomorrow if Iris was still sick. If not, they could still eat roast chicken.

While the soup heated, she pulled out the chicken, putting it in a bowl of cold water.

She felt someone behind her and turned to see Adam. He'd been reading upstairs.

"Something wrong with Iris?"

"She seems to have caught the swim team bug, and I'm not allowed to hover."

"Sounds like Iris, all right. Got a TV table set up for her?"

She shook her head. "Didn't think of it yet."

He smiled crookedly. "Tell you what. You go set up the table and I'll bring the soup, okay?"

"Then we'll both be hovering."

"She'll have to deal with it."

Fair division of labor, Jazz decided. Fair division of Iris's objections.

Once they had Iris seated at her soup, Jazz suggested some TV to entertain her.

"At this time of day? All that's on is the news and the weather. I know what the weather is." Sheba had come to rest right beside Iris's chair, and Iris reached down to pet her briefly. The dog's tail wagged a couple of times.

Jazz's smile widened. "Cricket is on."

"Cricket?" Iris looked appalled. "That's boring."

"Not at all. Compared to a baseball game a T20 is faster. It requires real strategy. And what's more, there are no pinch hitters or substitute pitchers. Eleven players to a team, all of them have to be able to bat and field, and only five bowlers are chosen in each team."

"You're going to have to explain." But Iris looked interested.

"I'll sit here and explain if you want. Trust me, this makes baseball look slow."

"That's not hard to do," Adam remarked. "I'm game. Let's turn it on." He looked at Jazz. "How did you discover this?"

"Not exactly a discovery," she replied, picking up the remote. "I have a friend from India and he got me intrigued. Then he insisted I go with him to the exhibition game played every year in Lauderdale by international players. I got very much hooked."

"What two teams play?" Iris asked as Jazz pulled up the guide on the screen.

"Not teams the way you think of them, at least not usually. Cricket is played all over the world, and except in international competitions where they represent their countries, teams are made up of players from everywhere."

Pale as she was looking, Iris appeared to approve of that idea. "Let's go, but you better be prepared to do a lot of explaining."

Jazz laughed. "Someone had to teach me, too. I'm not sure I get it all yet. But I'll give it a try." She turned on a game that had already begun and got ready to talk. It was going to require a lot of talking.

AN HOUR LATER, as the Indian Premier League game reached a close, Jazz looked at the time. "Oh my gosh! I forgot all about dinner!"

"I've got it," Adam said, rising. He headed for the hallway.

Jazz followed as Iris attempted to watch the interviews after the game. Her niece was a quick study and seemed to have picked up quite a bit in the half of the match they had seen.

"Are you going out?" she asked Adam as he pulled his jacket on.

"Not for long. I'll pick up dinner at Maude's. But I better ask everyone what they want. Especially our sick girl."

Surprisingly for an ill young woman, Iris asked, "Can I eat something bad, Aunt Jazz?"

"I'm not your coach. Besides, you're not feeling well. Have whatever you want."

A few minutes later, Adam headed out the door after explaining some of the selections to Jazz. He'd written the choices on a scrap of paper.

"We're all going to eat the wrong things tonight," Iris said.

"I'm astonished that you'll break your training diet for anything."

"It won't be the first time." Iris closed her eyes. "I think I need a nap."

Jazz started for the kitchen when she spied the mail Iris had dumped unsorted on the hall table. She went to complete the task, peeling away all the sales flyers, offers of lower-rate mortgages, and reminders that it was about time someone had a dental checkup.

Then she came to the handwritten postcard and gasped. Her knees suddenly felt like water.

*I'm watching you.*

JAZZ SAID NOTHING about the postcard when Adam returned with dinner. With Iris in the house, it seemed like exactly the wrong time to bring up this mess.

Iris looked at the foam container on the TV table and remarked, "Foam is bad for the environment."

Adam regarded her. "Then *you* talk to Maude about it."

Iris gave a weary laugh. "I'm not brave enough."

"I don't think anyone would be."

Jazz spoke, trying to keep her mind off the postcard although discomfort filled her. "Is she a dragon?"

"Next best thing," Iris answered.

"But she still has customers?"

Iris shrugged. "We're all used to it."

"And the food is great," Adam reminded her. "The food more than makes up for service…which can be quite entertaining."

"It's a wonder she doesn't break more cups and plates," Iris remarked. "The way she bangs them down."

"Probably made of painted cast iron."

Iris laughed tiredly at the joke, then sighed. "I guess I'm not used to being sick."

"Do you feel too bad to eat?" Jazz asked.

Iris started to shake her head, then winced. "My

head aches. My body aches. I feel so tired. But nothing's wrong with my stomach."

"Then go for it," Adam said.

Jazz spoke. "How about some dishes to eat off?"

"I won't be able to wash them, Aunt Jazz."

"And I'm incapable of popping things in the dishwasher? Puh-leeze."

Another weak laugh from Iris. "No plate necessary. The box is part of the fun."

As if the girl was going to have much fun eating from the look of her, Jazz thought. She wondered if she should do something more, like drag Iris to the doctor. She wasn't that familiar with illness herself.

But the thought of dragging Iris to a doctor was daunting. Her niece would have to feel a whole lot worse to agree.

Strike one for being a mere aunt.

"I'll be okay, Aunt Jazz," Iris said as if she read Jazz's face. "Really."

Jazz smiled faintly. "How'd I know you'd say that?"

"Because you're getting to know me. Now you guys go eat in the kitchen. The dining room table is a mess and using your laps won't be any fun."

Reluctantly Jazz followed Adam to the kitchen.

"I think she wants to be alone," Adam remarked. "No hovering, remember?"

"All too well."

Jazz slid her container onto the table and put the thawing chicken into the refrigerator while

Adam went to make another pot of coffee. He really seemed to like it.

"It was nice of you to run out and pick up dinner."

"Like any of us was in a mood for cooking. The only thing I didn't like was leaving you guys alone. Maude probably never had such an impatient customer."

Jazz was about to tell him once again that he didn't have to disrupt his life, but there *was* that postcard, bright red in her mind for all it was just a basic white card. The third warning that something was happening. Threatening.

Before she opened her meal, she went to get the card. It sounded as if Iris was still watching cricket, but maybe she'd fallen asleep. She might need that more than food.

When she got back to the kitchen, she sat down with Adam who was just opening his meal.

"This came in the mail today."

He reached across the table and took the card. "It's addressed to Lily."

"Turn it over. The back side was up when I saw it."

He read the words printed on the back and frowned deeply. "This is no joke. Especially not when you've been feeling watched. I'll tell the Chief about this."

She nodded. "I'm wound so tight now I don't feel like eating."

"Eat anyway. Just a little. God almighty, what's going on here?"

Jazz doubted she could pick up a fork, let alone swallow anything. Her stomach felt as if a rock filled it.

"Come on, just one french fry," Adam coaxed. "Bland. Safe, soft. The meat probably looks like too much just now."

It certainly did. But he'd gone to all the trouble to get the food, and she hated to be rude. Just one fry. Maybe that would get her started.

Adam put the card on the table to one side and began to eat his own meal. "It's postmarked from Cheyenne."

Jazz gave him a hopeful look. "That's far away, isn't it?"

"Not that far. Just eat, Jazz. We can beat our heads on this later."

She reached for another fry, to please him, and discovered that a bit of her appetite had returned. Maybe he was right. Starving herself wouldn't help anyone, least of all Iris.

"This guy," she said, "is an SOB"

"Yeah."

Jazz looked at the food in front of her and decided it was time to dig in.

ANDY ROBBINS WAITED in Cheyenne. He had more postcards to send, increasingly frightening, he hoped. But right now he didn't want to hang around in Conard City too much.

What had persuaded Lily to move to such a small place? Iris must be bored to death. It wasn't Lily's kind of place either, as evidenced by her jetting all over the world now. And she'd always liked things to do from art museums to concerts to night clubs.

When he was willing to let her go, at least. Museums bored him and the concerts she chose rarely appealed to him.

But he smiled as he remembered the times he'd stopped her. Sometimes with a blow or two. Women had to be kept in line.

But mostly he wouldn't let her see her friends. She might have talked to them.

Not that Andy had done anything wrong. Just being a strong husband, doing his job. Anyway, he didn't like it when Lily screwed up. When she made him furious.

No woman had the right to do that to a man. *No* woman.

Well, now was the time to make her regret it.

## Chapter Nine

Adam was seriously disturbed by this campaign of terror. It made him furious on Jazz's behalf and worried on behalf of Iris. His urge to violence had pretty much died in the war, but he was feeling it right then. He wanted to take someone out with his bare fists. Grab him by the throat.

But he was looking at a ghost enemy. Unknown. So far unknowable other than that he had some fixation on Lily. Or a grudge. But what could it be? Adam had known Lily during the years since she had moved to Conard City. A very pleasant, very smooth woman who clearly knew how *not* to offend. Part of her job, he supposed, but of one thing he was fairly certain: those who knew her in this town liked her.

While Lily might have been an alien species to the kind of folks who lived here, she had managed to fit herself in, globe-trotting or not. Iris had almost instantly fit right in.

Now this. An unmistakable threat. Judging by the squirrel, it was a threat of violence.

Adam had seen the worst of human nature so little surprised him. But Lily had been frank about choosing a small town so her daughter could live freely and without fear.

With a few exceptions in the past, that was true for all the kids here.

Now this.

He needed to get out and run a few miles. Or get to his personal gym. But he didn't want to leave Iris and Jazz alone. No way. And what about his vets support group tomorrow evening? He'd have to skip that along with his exercise.

Later, when he was alone upstairs, he swore. He wanted to pace his room but didn't want Jazz to hear. Downstairs was off-limits for making any real noise because Iris had fallen asleep in the living room, having eaten only a small part of her dinner. Continued pacing would likely disturb her.

Crap! Well, since he wasn't going to sleep, he might as well hunt up something to eat or drink. He could do that quietly and gnawing on some food was better than gnawing on his fists.

In stocking feet, he descended the stairs taking care to step near the wall to minimize any creaks. He carried his boots with him. Nobody who'd been a soldier wanted to be caught barefoot when action was required.

He saw light spilling from the kitchen as he descended, so he wasn't surprised when he discovered Jazz at the table, chin in her hand, her expression weary.

"Can't sleep?" he asked as she looked up.

"Hardly. You either?"

"Nope."

"There's a bottomless coffee pot," she told him. "Not to mention leftovers from dinner and a whole bunch of Iris-friendly snacks if you'd prefer fruit."

"Coffee won't help either of us sleep," he remarked as he chose an apple from a wire basket on the counter.

"At this point I don't care. I keep wondering what's next."

"Hard not to wonder." He bit into the apple as he sat facing her. It provided a satisfying crunch and a mouthful of juice. "Iris?"

"Still soundly asleep with the dog beside her. Nice of you to share Sheba with her."

Adam shrugged. "Sheba knows how to find me if I need her. That dog is half Iris's anyway."

"So it appears."

He noticed that Jazz didn't even try to smile. Too tired and worried to try to lift the corners of her mouth, he guessed. He couldn't blame her.

Here she was in a strange place with her niece dependent on her. Quite a load of responsibility when things were going wrong.

"You must have jobs you need to do," she remarked.

"Nothing on my schedule. Folks know how to reach my cell if they have an emergency." Although what the hell he'd do about it if someone truly needed him he couldn't imagine. No leaving these two on their own.

His hip had started aching again, and while he was usually able to bury the pain, tonight it bit him and refused to be ignored. Ibuprofen, maybe.

Perhaps he'd been trying too hard not to limp so Jazz wouldn't ask him about it. It was a bad reminder of Afghanistan, a subject he avoided.

Jazz spoke. "I wish I knew how to corral Iris more without letting her know how scared I am for her."

"I don't want to scare her either. And this threat seems to be directed at Lily."

"From the postcard, yes. From the other stuff I'm not so sure."

Neither was he, but he didn't want to say so. Jazz was already upset enough.

"Maybe I should call Lily."

Adam immediately shook his head. "She's half a world away. Nothing she can do about this. No reason to scare her."

"But she might have an idea who could be…" Then Jazz shook her head. "What would she do anyway? Answer questions on the phone then continue with her work? Not likely." She knew her sister too well. Lily would race home, race into town hell-for-leather, and probably be just as stymied as they were. Adam was right. No need to scare her.

She sighed and sipped the coffee she shouldn't be drinking at this hour. He decided to join her. What the hell. Sleep had decided to skip town, leaving them both wide awake.

Eventually she spoke. "We've got to do something."

"I don't know what at this point. We don't know who's doing this or why. We need more to go on. Any suggestions?"

Jazz had none, of course. How could she? That was the wall they were both up against.

The night passed slowly as they both dealt with their inner worries.

Jazz wanted to crawl out of her skin. Drag herself and Iris into a dark hole for safety. But Adam had been right when he said that they needed to try to solve this before Lily came home. If they could before something terrible happened.

And that postcard, still sitting on the table, seemed to emphasize that someone meant to terrify Lily.

Not that Lily could be terrified easily, except probably when it came to Iris. Jazz had long admired Lily's strength, far more than her own. She had never been tested the way Lily had.

Thank God.

Now her sister was running around the world, a highly respected consultant to various entities, from the World Bank to the UN. She'd always had the smarts.

Not that Jazz thought poorly of herself. She'd never have been able to write books if she didn't have a measure of self-confidence. *Her* babies went out into the world to be liked or disliked, criticized or lauded. She'd long ago decided that critiques, positive or negative, were merely a single person's opinion. What really talked were sales numbers, the numbers her career rose or fell by.

She wanted to walk to the window, to look out at a normal world, but she had the curtains drawn against the night. Against the possibility than anyone could look in and see.

Against the threat that so far seemed to lie outside these walls. With Adam in here, she felt safer. He'd shaken up his entire life to come riding over here like the cavalry. She doubted many would do that.

He kept moving in his chair, not as if he were anxious, but as if he were uncomfortable.

"Is something wrong?" she asked.

"With me? Not really. My hip just hurts too much to ignore sometimes."

"I'm sorry. Old injury?"

"Not old enough, apparently. Putting it back together didn't make it much happier."

"That's awful." She bit her lip then asked, "How?"

"How did it happen? The war. Others have it a lot worse."

Which closed the discussion, Jazz decided. Maybe she'd walked into private places. Maybe she had reminded him of terrible things. If so, this situation had to be awful for him.

She knew he was a vet, but she'd never really considered how this might affect him. Now she felt awful about him, too.

"It's okay, Jazz," he said as if he could read her face.

Well, he probably could. She'd often been told her face was an open book. "It's not okay. How could it be? You shouldn't have to go through that. No one should."

"Well, I put on the uniform."

"Sure. As if you had any idea what you were getting into."

"Most people don't. It doesn't matter. I made a choice. I live with the consequences, like everyone else."

A remarkably strong and clear-eyed view. She wasn't sure she agreed with him, however, but she couldn't argue with him.

Silence fell again, echoed by the quiet night outside.

Eventually he spoke. "There'll be more postcards. Brace yourself."

She started. "How can you be sure of that?"

"Because this guy is a coward. If he wasn't, he'd come out in the open and do whatever it is he's fantasizing. He wants to scare, not to act. At least not yet."

"Yet?" She hated the sound of that word.

"He's ginning himself up bit by bit. Telling himself he's enjoying the fear he's engendering, but do you see him at the front door actually *doing* something? He's giving us time, whether he knows it or not. Time to prepare. Maybe time to find out who he is."

"Well that's hopeful," she said a bit sarcastically. "So far he's good at covering his tracks."

"So far. But I'm a great believer in people making mistakes even in threatening situations. I've seen enough of it. He'll make a mistake."

"I hope."

He went to get more coffee and another apple. "Want anything?"

"A huge piece of cheesecake or a cinnamon roll. The more sugar the better."

He smiled faintly. "Can't do anything about that right now, although I think you'll find some sugar in the pantry."

Miserable as she was, Jazz summoned her own smile. "Just a spoonful, right? Like that song."

"Oh, live a little and take two."

Out of context though it was, Adam was lifting her spirits. Just a bit. She was grateful to him.

"So," he said as he sat again, wincing slightly as if he were trying not to reveal his discomfort. "Here we sit, two people faced with a situation and no control. I hate it when I don't have control."

"I feel the same. But what's that saying? If you want to make God laugh, make a plan."

"Too true. But we can't even make a plan yet." His face hardened. "We'll get there, I swear."

She believed him, believed Adam would move heaven and earth to protect her and Iris. Mostly Iris, the main concern for both of them.

As if summoned, Sheba arrived to nuzzle Adam's arm, then rest her chin on his thigh.

"Good girl," he murmured as he stroked her head and back.

In that moment Jazz saw another side of Adam. A gentle, soft side.

*Sheba will come when I need her.*

Evidently he needed her now, and Jazz was surprised when he bent over to drop a kiss on the dog's head.

Sheba raised her head to look adoringly at Adam, then licked his face with a kiss of her own. He'd said she comforted him, and apparently that's what she was doing now.

He continued to pet her, fondling her ears a bit.

Jazz wondered what Sheba had sensed that she had not. Just a minute ago she'd been thinking that Adam would move heaven and earth for Iris and her, and now the dog sensed a need.

Memories brought on by this mess somehow. Jazz couldn't imagine what this situation had to do with war, unless it was the tension. Or that hip of his.

"Need some ibuprofen?" she asked.

Adam looked up from the dog. "I've been thinking about it since I got down here."

"Thinking is not the same as action. I'll get it for you."

Jazz brought him the bottle so he could decide how much to take. A doctor had once told her that she could take as many as four at a time for her migraines, as long as it didn't upset her stomach. "There's prescription ibuprofen that strong. Take what you need, just don't exceed four every six hours."

She saw Adam pop four tablets. She suspected he could have used something stronger, but who could get that now?

"How bad is it, Adam? And don't brush me off."

"Nerve damage," he said. "Joint damage. Maybe a hip replacement down the road." He shrugged. "I can still live with it."

That said a lot. *Still live with it.* "That's awful."

He shook his head. "As they say, it is what it is."

"You can say that about a lot of things, but it doesn't make them any easier to endure." Rising, she decided that sleep was a lost cause and went to get her own coffee. It had started to smell burnt, so she dumped it and began a new pot.

"We're both going to be useless tomorrow."

Still stroking Sheba, he nodded. "Except I'm used to functioning without sleep."

"I'm not. It's going to show."

"So sleep when you can. I'll hold the fort. And I'm going to stash that card so Iris doesn't see it until I can pass it to the law."

"I was thinking the same thing." She reached for the pot. "Want some fresh?"

"Oh, yeah. I got through a lot of nights on caffeine. Wasn't as good as this brewed stuff, though."

Jazz wrinkled her nose. "My dad used to drink instant. He traveled a lot so he had one of those heaters you could put in a mug to boil the water. I thought it was a horrible habit."

He smiled. "You get used to it."

"You can get used to a lot. Doesn't mean it's good."

He chuckled. "Got it in one."

Then the quiet fell again, the night seeming to creep into the room. Sheba finally lay down beside Adam's chair, still there in case she was needed.

Loyalty thy name is dog, Jazz thought.

The night would slip away soon, leaving dawn in its wake. Would it be gray and misty again? She didn't much care now, but it seemed apropos to the events. As if the sky shared their concerns.

It was a foolish thought, but it fit nicely into her writer's brain. Possibilities could be endless in her fantasy books.

In this world not so much.

Like right now. In one of her worlds, the trees would be whispering information. In another the very rocks might have an opinion. In this reality she and Adam were stuck waiting for a creep to make a misstep.

"Why don't you go try to lie down?" Adam said.

Which made her aware for the first time that her eyes were closing. Just a bit. Then anxiety would snap her awake again.

"I don't think so," she said after a minute. She wondered if she'd ever sleep again, not with anxiety slapping her every few minutes.

"Take some long, deep, slow breaths. It'll help relieve the tension."

She took his advice and soon realized that he was right. Physically she relaxed, although her mind didn't seem ready to slow down.

"We can't keep this up," she said.

"No we can't." He rose and brought them both fresh cups of brew. "I could use a beer right about now."

"Like you can find some any easier than I can get my cinnamon roll."

He winked. "There's a place just across the street, namely my house, which usually holds a six-pack."

"Then go get it."

He shook his head, and that was the end of that.


RARELY COULD EX-CONS find a job. Not that Andy had often held one. Lily's income had made it unnecessary and he didn't mind living off her earnings. They were pretty comfortable.

But something had happened to her. When he'd met Lily she'd been so ready to please him, quivering anytime he got annoyed with her. He hadn't needed to do much to keep her in line at first.

It pleased her to please him. A simple recipe for marital happiness. While he kept her from her friends, and mostly from her family such as it was, he didn't keep her from work. She was rising rapidly, proud of every new accomplishment.

He'd let her have that pride because it suited him. But then she got out of line a bit. Just before Iris. Damn, he'd hated that pregnancy. It meant there'd be a third person in their tightly controlled loop.

He'd tried to talk Lily into an abortion. Then he'd knocked her around to teach her to listen to him. Then it was too late and that kid was coming anyway.

Only after the brat was born had he realized he had a new method of controlling Lily. He'd told himself that he could make Lily behave in order to protect the baby because, as he knew too well, Lily was a selfish bitch.

Iris. Stupid name. That whole family had stupid ideas about names. Anyway, Iris had given him the excuse to threaten Lily into cutting away the remnants of her life: her family, her friends. A complete separation after that, keeping Lily from bad influences.

A threat to make Lily behave. Iris became a useful tool, often more useful than his fists. Although he still got a lot of pleasure out of hitting the woman every now and then. It was like a pressure relief valve.

But he'd had a lot of time in prison to reconstruct his images of the past. Lily had always been disobedient, treating him like crap. He'd been the injured party.

As for Iris, in his mind he'd built a loving relationship with her. *He'd* been the one to prevent Lily from having an abortion. He'd stood up for the kid, then protected her from Lily.

He believed he'd used every means he could to make Lily into a good wife.

She'd failed him and deserved everything that came her way.

As for Iris, he'd protect her as he always had.

## Chapter Ten

Iris still felt ill in the morning. All she wanted for breakfast was toast with a bit of jam.

Jazz hated to admit that she was almost relieved that Iris would be home for another day. One day she needn't worry about her niece racketing around out there without any protection except her friends.

The sun had decided to wake that morning, and Iris seemed glad to have it brightening the world again. So was Jazz for that matter.

"I'm going to run across the street," Adam said while Jazz made toast. "I'll be quick, but I need a few things."

"The washer and dryer work," she said drily.

He laughed quietly. "I don't just need some clean clothes."

"Then don't forget the beer."

"I won't. If you feel okay about it, I may make a quick run downtown."

"I'll survive. We'll survive. Go."

"No more than half an hour," he said. He was

going to do his best imitation of the winged god Mercury. "Lock up everything behind me. And Sheba can stay with Iris."

"You sure?" Jazz asked. She remembered his apparent need for the dog.

"Running helps. Trust me."

She wondered how it could possibly help his hip.

ADAM TOOK OFF as if the hounds of hell were on his heels. He didn't take his dirty clothes with him; Jazz was right that there was a washer and dryer over at Lily's house. He had a different errand in mind.

People waved as he dashed past, but no one gave him an odd look. Most folks around here were used to the sight of him running along the street at top speed. A mere jog wouldn't always help him. Now it wouldn't be fast enough to get back to his ladies.

He was starting to think of them as *his*. Oh man. He put it down to feeling so protective.

As fast as he was moving, he reached the bakery swiftly. Nearly a four-minute mile, he calculated. Not bad for a guy in his condition. He ignored the screaming of his hip.

He wasn't a frequent visitor to the bakery, but Melinda welcomed him with a warm smile and called him by name. Benefit of a small town.

She filled a couple of white bags for him, with Danish and cinnamon rolls and chocolate chip cookies.

"That enough?" she asked wryly.

"Ladies at home with a craving."

Melinda laughed. "That'll do it." Then she asked, "Are you running?"

"Yeah. Feels good."

"Then wait a sec."

Next thing he knew, she'd put the white bags in a larger paper bag with handles. "Now you can hang on to it."

"You're the best."

Then he was out the door at a full run, making a swing by the grocery where he bought plenty of chicken soup, subs for everyone—one a chicken salad out of deference to Iris's illness. If she wanted a meatier one with all the trimmings, he'd eat the chicken salad.

A six-pack of beer rounded out his purchases.

The lady at the register, Doris, eyed him. "You look like you're running again."

"Rumor has it."

She smiled and surprised him with large plastic-handled bags, doubled up. She even put the bakery bag safely on the top. "I don't know how you thought you were going to run all this home."

"Somehow," he answered, giving her a grin.

"Yeah. You soldiers, always biting off more than you can carry. Get going before you get stiff."

His hip really would have liked a heating pad, but he continued to ignore it. Jazz and Iris were home alone and the awareness gnawed at him.

So far, the creep who was sending messages

struck him like a coward. The kind who would attack only those smaller and physically weaker. Adam was at least big enough to make him reconsider if he had more in mind than creating fear.

Just a little more than thirty minutes. Not bad. He used the key Lily had given him for emergencies to unlock the door.

Sheba appeared immediately, dancing around his legs with a rapidly wagging tail.

He heard Iris say, "My hair looks like a rat's nest."

"If that's your only worry," Jazz answered, "then you're doing pretty darn good."

"I don't want to miss the swim practice this afternoon."

"If you think the other sick girls are going to be in any better condition, I've got a bridge to sell you."

Adam smiled as he passed the living room and entered the kitchen. He began to unload the bags when he heard Jazz step through the door.

"What in the world did you do, Adam?"

"Went on a shopping spree. After a sleepless night, nobody's going to feel like cooking."

She joined him and helped with the groceries. "You got that right. If I didn't feel like I was getting an electric shock every few minutes, I'd be unconscious on the floor."

"The creep's got to you that much?" A stupid question considering he hadn't slept last night either.

He grabbed ibuprofen and settled at the table with a beer. Always five o'clock somewhere as the saying went. Although he didn't care with the jackhammer pain in his hip. "It's still chilly out there, especially for you Southerners."

Tossing him a tired smile, Jazz opened the bakery bags. "Oh my God, Adam! What did you do?"

"Somebody mentioned a craving last night." He shrugged, dismissing it, although her reaction pleased him.

"But this is so much! I can't eat it all. Nor will Iris since she seems to have remembered her training diet. Apples and oranges and bananas."

"Well, if she doesn't help you eat this, I'll take care of it."

"You think you're capable?" She sat facing him. "How were you so fast? I didn't see you drive away."

"I ran. I told you."

"But this fast?" she repeated. "When do you show up in the Olympics?"

"Never." He changed the subject. "How's Iris doing? If she's complaining about her hair, she has to be feeling better."

"I'm not sure about that. I think she's impatient to get over this bug. If her color was better, I'd agree with you. I keep wondering if I should take her to the doctor."

"So the doc can say there's a bug going around? Besides, you'd probably have to hog-tie that girl to get her to go."

"I was thinking of that."

He arched a brow. "You'd really hog-tie her?"

"Not hardly." She sighed. "I know nothing about this mother thing. I'm always worrying if I'm doing the wrong thing."

"Iris is still breathing, she hasn't needed a trip to the hospital, and she hasn't brought home a guy with a green Mohawk wearing chains and leather."

She cocked a brow at him. "He might be perfectly nice."

"Then ask yourself why he isn't advertising that. Now go have one of those pastries. You were jonesing last night. I'll go see if Iris wants one."

He tossed his beer bottle in the trash and Sheba followed him to the living room.

HER HEART ONLY half in it, Jazz looked through the pastry bags and decided on a cinnamon roll. A very big one. She was past caring about her weight. She poured some coffee to go with it, then sat again, thinking Adam was one heck of a nice guy.

Running all the way to the bakery? Because she'd wished for a pastry in the middle of the night? Not many people would do that. Or would even remember her crazy wish, probably born of fatigue. Weariness could make people hungry, she'd heard. Regardless, she might not have tasted the roll at all except for the cinnamon.

The postcard was gone from the table, but not

her memory of it. How could anyone have it in for Lily? Enough to go on a campaign of terror?

The only person she could think of was Lily's ex-husband, Andy, but he was still in prison. Safely locked away.

Jazz had been stunned when she'd found out what Lily had been enduring. She'd wondered why Lily had been growing more distant but had put it down to Lily's preoccupation with her new family, especially Iris.

Then the horror had tumbled out once Andy was arrested. All of it. Sickening to the last detail. The only thing Jazz wanted to ask was why Lily had endured it for so long, but she never asked.

Instead she'd hit the books and learned just how corrosive living with an abuser could be. How damaging to self-esteem. How terrified of a man's anger. Then there was Iris, protecting Iris from the man.

Except the protection had finally run out and Iris had been hurt. Lily had snapped then and headed straight to the police. Jazz was convinced to this day that Andy had gotten his just desserts only because of Iris. That poor little girl. Enough to wring anyone's heart.

Jazz had been there for Lily and Iris from the moment she learned about the abuse, and all the way through the trial and sentencing. X-rays of broken bones, on both Lily and the child. No photos of bruising until it came to Iris.

Lily had explained her own injuries away, probably from fear, but she hadn't explained Iris's away. No, from the first moment at the hospital she'd told the staff of Andy's physical abuse of the girl.

There'd been therapy, of course. Iris appeared to recover quickly. Lily had taken longer, but she'd gone back to work with a vengeance, rising high and rising quickly, as if she'd been held back during her marriage. Maybe she had.

Regardless, work had improved Lily's self-esteem immeasurably. Now years had passed and both she and Iris seemed to have recovered completely, although who knew what nightmares Lily might have in the dead of the night, nightmares she kept to herself.

She heard Iris and Adam talking, Iris sounding as upbeat as she could possibly manage when feeling ill. Then Adam returned.

"I turned Sheba over to Iris. That girl is going to steal her from me. Anyway, she said a cheese Danish sounds good."

"I'll take her one."

He gave her a crooked smile. "Hovering?"

"Checking in. Which I think I'm entitled to do." She realized she sounded snappish but felt no need to apologize. Lack of sleep, a horrendous level of anxiety, and not being able to close her eyes without seeing dead flowers, a gutted squirrel and that postcard. It would make anyone irritable—or worse.

Adam might be right that the guy was a coward, but that wasn't preventing him from inflicting fear.

She went to the living room only to find Iris sound asleep. That was good, she supposed. Rest could help almost anything.

Adam came in behind her and spoke in a hushed voice. "Try to nap. I'll be right here. You've got to sleep sometime."

"What about you?"

"If I sleep, I'm a very light sleeper. Any noise will wake me. Truly. Now go to bed. As tired as you are, I bet you fall asleep in two minutes. I'll stay on the couch in case *I* do."

She couldn't argue with him. Her eyes felt gritty and she wasn't at all sure she was thinking clearly.

Okay. She'd have to believe what he'd said about being a light sleeper, and given where he'd been, he was probably telling the truth.

The instant her head hit the pillow, she was out like a light.

ADAM SAT ON the other recliner, remaining upright. He'd probably doze some, but he hadn't been kidding. The slightest abnormal sound could wake him in an instant. And when it did, he'd become wide awake.

Lessons of war. War taught a lot of lessons, not often good ones.

So far he was pretty sure this creep wasn't likely to act. More postcards, probably. Maybe another ugly, gutted animal. Scare tactics. But why?

He couldn't imagine Lily having engendered that

kind of hate in anyone. Just couldn't imagine it. There were people in this town who had enemies. But none of *them* would ever stoop to such heinous acts. They usually just ignored each other, had verbal fights and the occasional swinging of fists.

Pretty much normal reactions, the latter especially when drunk. Occasionally Mahoney's bar enjoyed the inebriated results.

The cops would break up the fights if necessary, someone might spend a night in the holding cell above the sheriff's offices, but that was usually the extent of it. As long as no one got seriously hurt, why make a criminal case out of it?

Not necessary in this small town. People got drunk, threw a couple of punches, many of which missed their targets. He'd seen it happen more than once.

In a way, it amused him. Not a proper outlet for anger, but still amusing.

This was a whole different kettle of fish.

He sighed and looked over at Iris. She still slept but looked a bit flushed. Maybe because she was buried under a blanket. On the small side table a plate held an untouched cheese Danish.

He'd keep an eye on her, too, in case she worsened.

But Lily? This had to be a person from her past, someone she never mentioned. Deciding he needed to question Jazz, he dozed too, confident in his ability to wake.

Sleep needed its due sometimes.

JAZZ SLEPT LATER than she wanted, the late afternoon sun peeking through an edge of the curtain. She didn't practice her usual routine of allowing herself to wake slowly but sat bolt upright and scrambled for some clean clothes. To hell with a shower for now. She was sure she didn't stink yet.

She headed straight for the living room and there was Adam, wide awake. She then looked at Iris, who was sitting up too, and who hadn't touched the Danish.

Without preamble, Jazz said, "How are you feeling?"

"Awful," came the frank, tired answer.

"I should take you to the doctor."

"A waste of money," Iris argued.

Thus the fight began. "I'm worried about you."

"Oh, for heaven's sake! The swim team probably got it from someone at school, half the kids are sick and nobody's gone to the hospital. If they had I'd have heard about it." Iris waved her cell phone. "No alerts. No messages. Nada."

"Iris…"

"Nope. I'll live. I'll just be miserable for a while."

The mulish look on the girl's face told Jazz that Adam had been right: she'd have to hog-tie Iris.

All she could do was sigh. "You hungry?"

"Not really. Come on, Aunt Jazz. I'll live."

Then Iris leaned back in the chair, clearly fatigued.

Adam spoke. "Did she get that stubbornness from you?"

"And Lily," Jazz answered. "But I know when I'm beat."

Cricket reruns still ran across the TV screen. "I like this game," Iris remarked. "How come I never heard about it before?"

"I told you, Americans think it's boring."

Iris blew air between her lips. "Well, there was a time no one liked soccer because the scores were too low. It'll change."

"Want some chicken soup?" Jazz asked hopefully. "You need to keep up your energy to fight this bug."

"Sure," came a distracted answer as Iris returned to her fascination with the game on the TV.

Jazz headed for the kitchen. Adam joined her. "Coffee?" he asked.

"Yes, please." She found one of the cans of chicken soup Adam had bought that morning— had it been just the morning?—and started it on the stove.

"Are *you* feeling any better?" Adam asked.

"A whole lot. You?"

"I got some catnapping in. Although when I was young we had a cat who took her time about waking up, complete with half-open eyes and yawns. No catnaps for her. She slept like a log."

Jazz actually chuckled. "Unique."

"Definitely one of a kind."

"What was her name?"

"Tabby. I was a creative seven-year-old. Not."

"I think it's a cute name."

"You and eight million other people."

Jazz took the soup to Iris in a large cappuccino cup. Less likely to spill. "Want some company?"

"You go talk to Adam. And give Sheba back to him. Evidently I've monopolized her."

"The dog has two homes."

Iris managed a smile. "Yup."

Sheba was willing to follow when Jazz called her, and greeted Adam with adoring eyes and a tail that wagged fast enough to helicopter her from the ground.

"You've been babysitting today, haven't you, girl. I think it's time to take you out back." Adam looked at Jazz. "I'll scoop the backyard, so don't worry about it."

"I hadn't even considered it." Which was true.

Out the back window, she saw Adam and Sheba playing fetch with the tennis ball. Now that he thought he was unobserved, Adam limped visibly.

God, he probably shouldn't have been running around town today. Then she remembered the chicken in the fridge and hard on the thought's heels, she also remembered the subs Adam had bought. Plenty of pastry, too.

She helped herself to another cinnamon roll and poured her coffee.

When Adam returned, he fed the dog and filled a

bowl with water. Then he grabbed a stack of cookies, a cup of coffee, and sat.

"Ibuprofen," she said.

He arched a brow.

"I saw you outside. Maybe you have to put up with some suffering, but whatever helps ease it."

"Orders?"

"You got it. In fact, I'll get the tablets and you stay put." She retrieved the bottle from the cupboard, got him a glass of water, then plopped both on the table beside him.

"Mothering me?"

"I doubt you need it." She waved at his water glass. "My great-grandmother used to keep a bottle of water in the fridge at all times. I loved it."

"But your parents didn't?"

Jazz snorted. "The refrigerator was always too full, according to Mom, but heaven forfend anyone took too much ice."

"Dang."

Jazz shrugged. "Just the way it was. I'm an ice fiend now."

"Living where you do? I'm hardly surprised." He hesitated visibly. "Jazz, I was wondering?"

She waited.

"Nobody around here has the least reason to do this kind of thing to Lily, so I was wondering if someone from her past might."

Jazz didn't want to get into this. It might be betraying Lily's confidence. And what if Adam didn't understand the psychology of an abused woman? Many people didn't, simply demanding to know why the woman hadn't left her abuser sooner. They didn't know how slowly it began, how it undermined the woman's confidence. How it left her feeling responsible for every blow. How it made her feel that she deserved it.

She decided to anyway, believing Adam could be made to understand if he didn't immediately.

"Her ex-husband," Jazz said hesitantly. "He's in prison for abusing her and Iris."

"Dear God in heaven!"

For the first time, Jazz saw Adam look shocked. Really shocked.

"Oh my God," he said after a few seconds. "The two of them?"

"I always thought the X-rays of Iris were the clincher for the jury. A lot of people don't understand why a woman doesn't walk out. But those X-rays were heart-wrenching. Apparently, Andy had been using Iris as a threat to keep Lily in line. Then he went too far."

Adam just shook his head. "I can't think what to say. But you're sure he's in prison?"

"Florida doesn't have early release. Except in a few exceptional cases where the state might decide a prisoner has been on enough good behavior to get out after eighty-five percent of his sentence is complete. Takes some heavy-powered legal assistance to manage it, though. Almost everyone serves a full sentence."

"Wouldn't they have to tell her if they released him?"

"I don't know."

He swore again, drumming his fingers on the table, clearly thinking. He picked up a cookie and ate it. He drank coffee. Then he spoke. "It might explain a lot if he's out. Maybe I can get the sheriff to investigate. But abuse…isn't that all about control?"

"Control combined with a twisted mind."

He swore yet again, giving her a taste of an Army mouth. Quite a repertoire.

"Poor Lily. Poor Iris. God what a trial. You'd never guess now."

"They seem to have recovered," Jazz answered. "At least as well as they ever can."

He shook his head and ate another cookie. "I'm glad Lily isn't here."

"Me, too. I don't ever want to see her that terrified again. I feel awful that I never knew anything about it until she pressed charges."

"She was good at covering up, I take it. Even with her twin?"

"Clearly. I didn't see much of her at the time. She always had an excuse. The job, Iris, going out somewhere. I thought I understood. I guess not."

He shook his head and reached for another cookie. He stopped himself. "I have an eating disorder when I get really angry. Better than batter-ing holes in walls."

"By far." She felt awful for telling him about Andy. Not so much for Lily's privacy but because it had so visibly upset Adam. He was being so pro-tective of her and Iris. Wasn't that enough?

"Well," he said presently, we've definitely got to get to the root of this before Lily gets home. She's been through enough without fearing that some weirdo, any weirdo, might do that to her again."

Jazz agreed wholeheartedly. "But what can we do? We have no real clues. At least none that are useful."

"First thing is call the sheriff."

"Not the chief of police? What was his name?"

"Jake Madison. No, the sheriff. He's got more resources, and Jake would have to turn to him any-way. Might as well start at the top."

Now in Casper, Wyoming, Andy Robbins set him-self up in a homeless shelter, jockeying with other men in ragged clothing and dealing with the stench of unwashed bodies. At least this place had a group shower.

Meals were served with prayers, which Andy hated, but for food he'd put up with it in order to save his pocket change. Hitchhiking around this state was easier than he would have believed, but he didn't want to rent a car again too soon. The credit cards in his pocket were probably hot by now, and he needed to get a new one soon.

In the meantime, he spent a few bucks on another postcard and a stamp. Postmarked from a different place, a place that suggested he was getting closer to her. Lily would tighten like a spring.

Then there was Iris. Maybe he could use her to control Lily again. He didn't want to kill Lily. Oh, no. He wanted the satisfaction of terrifying her and beating her into line once more. She needed to understand that she'd never escape him, never defy him again. She was *his*.

Plus, she had to pay for his prison sentence. And he'd learned some damn useful tricks in there.

Smiling, he dropped the card in the mailbox outside the post office, smiling with anticipation of her reaction.

Savoring her growing fear.

But if terror didn't kick her back into line…well, he might just kill her.

No one else was going to ever have her. Sure as hell.

## Chapter Eleven

Iris began to feel better in the evening. She chose the chicken sub but asked Jazz to cut her just a quarter of it. "I'm not that hungry."

Being hungry at all was an improvement, Jazz thought. She began to feel relieved about that at least.

Unfortunately, the sheriff arrived while Iris was eating and there was no way to prevent Iris from knowing.

Gage Dalton presented an interesting figure, a visible hitch in his step, a burn scar covering his cheek that tugged up one corner of his mouth. There was a story there, Jazz thought, the writer in her trying to create one.

But Iris. She didn't want Iris to know about any of this unless it became unavoidable. Adam dealt with the problem.

"Got a sick young 'un here, Gage. Let's step outside. Jazz?"

She grabbed her jacket from the back of the

kitchen chair and joined both men on the end of the porch farthest from the living room window.

Gage studied Jazz for a few seconds. "You're not Lily, but damned if I wouldn't have thought so. Twins?"

Jazz nodded. "I'm Jasmine."

"What's happening?" Gage trained his dark gaze on Adam.

"Did Jake Madison talk to you?"

"About the flowers and the squirrel. He mentioned it. I didn't like it at all. He and his men have been keeping an eye out. Well, so have mine. Nothing seems unusual."

"Then we got this." Adam pulled the card from the inside pocket on his jacket.

Gage accepted it. "Damn it all to hell. Really?" Then he looked at the two of them. "Can I keep this?"

"Help yourself," Jazz answered. "I sure don't want it."

"Probably no identifiable prints on it," Gage remarked. "To many people handled it, including you two." He frowned deeply. "I don't like this any more than you. The flowers…maybe a sick joke. The squirrel, plain sick. But there's no mistaking the threat now. No way to brush it aside."

Adam agreed.

"You said you needed something from me?"

Jazz spoke. "From the card, we know the threat is directed at Lily."

Gage nodded agreement. "Nobody around here has a problem with her."

"That's why Adam asked about people in her past. There's one. Her ex was an abuser. Abused both her and Iris. Lily sent him to prison. He should still be there in Florida."

Gage nodded again. "Florida doesn't have any early release worth talking about, but I'll check." Now he shook his head. "You'd be amazed how much you can do while you're still inside of a prison."

Jazz felt a trickle of ice run down her spine. Her voice came out a whisper. "Meaning?"

"You get a friend who finishes his time before you. A friend willing to do a little chore for you."

Jazz's hand flew to her mouth. Suddenly she felt as if she couldn't breathe. "That's possible?"

"Not only in the movies," was Gage's grim response. "Okay, I've got a lot of investigating to do. All from a G-D postcard. Hell. I'll keep you posted."

With that, he turned and limped to the official Suburban parked on the street.

"He's good people. You'd never guess that when he arrived here, folks called him Hell's Own Archangel. But that's a story for another time." Adam looked at Jazz. "Let's get inside before Iris's curiosity overcomes her. I'll explain this."

"Be my guest."

She realized she was shaking only when she stepped indoors into the warmth. She didn't want to see Iris, not when she was this upset. Iris wouldn't miss it.

Instead she went to the kitchen and stood looking out the window, arms wrapped around herself, shivering. Andy might have sent someone from the *prison*? The problem, big enough before, had just grown huge. Gigantic. Now there'd be no way at all to identify this sleaze.

She felt a nudge against her leg and looked down. Sheba was staring up at her with liquid brown eyes. Evidently Sheba felt Jazz needed comforting. Nothing like the caring of a dog, she thought.

Unwrapping her arms, she squatted down and hugged the dog. "We'll get through this," she murmured into Sheba's scruff as her eyes dampened. "We will."

She heard Adam's step behind her. "Good news, Iris wants more of her sandwich and a diet soda. I'll take care of it." Then he snorted. "The damn pooch is playing nurse."

A watery laugh escaped Jazz. "So she is."

"You keep her for a while. I'll get her back soon enough."

"Yeah, when you need her. Maybe. If she isn't too busy."

"At the rate things are going, she's on full-time duty."

After looking after Iris, Adam took the dog out back to play fetch. It wasn't the biggest yard in the world, but it was enough for Sheba who got to run, turn around sharply, snap at the air and mainly sniff around for new and interesting smells. A very doggy time.

When they came in, Sheba sat in front of Adam.

"Treat time, huh?"

She wagged her tail.

"Okay, let's go get a few biscuits."

IRIS WANTED TO sleep in her own bed that night. Jazz was happy about it but insisted on following the girl up the stairs to make sure she was okay.

"Hovering again, Aunt Jazz. I'm feeling a whole lot better. Maybe I can get back to school and the team tomorrow."

"We'll see."

Iris blew her a raspberry.

Once her niece was safely tucked in bed, Jazz headed downstairs to find Adam pacing like a restless lion.

"Is something wrong?"

"Only that my hands are tied right now. Only that I have to wait for another shoe to drop. I'm not built for this."

"Is anyone? Pace away. I'll just enjoy the view."

That stopped him in midstride and seemed to nearly choke him. He faced her. "What?"

"You heard me." She gave him a lopsided smile. "There has to be something to enjoy right now. Anyway, I won't embarrass you. I'm going to have a piece of those subs you bought."

ADAM STOOD FOR a while, pacing forgotten. He felt a bit stunned by what Jazz had said, wondering what she meant. Nobody had ever said anything like that to him before, and he didn't know what to make of it. She couldn't possibly have been flirting with him. No way. Hell, given her fears for her sister and Iris, sex had to be the last thing on her mind.

She'd probably just been trying to distract him. Having someone pacing endlessly the way he was could be damned annoying.

The need for action ran along his every nerve ending. Patience had been required at times when he was in the military. Sitting in camouflage, covered in brambles and brush, waiting for an enemy. But that was different. He knew what was coming and why he had to wait. This time he had nothing except some vague threats. No direction, no idea of outcome. Not a foggy clue about whether Iris might be in danger.

He was seriously worried about Iris. Jazz, too, of course, but after what she'd told him about this Andy guy hurting the girl… Hell.

They couldn't lock Iris up like a bird in a cage. Not only would she fight it like mad and probably risk breaking her neck climbing out of her upstairs window, but they'd have to explain. She just wouldn't stand for it. Given the girl's breezy attitude toward life in general, she probably wouldn't believe *she* was in any danger. Nope. Besides the postcard had been addressed to Lily.

Iris would undoubtedly worry about her aunt but wouldn't see how she herself might be in danger.

Maybe he was making a mountain out of one molehill, but there wasn't enough to go on to avoid considering the possibility.

At last he wandered into the kitchen where Jazz had begun to eat half of her sub. He got his own from the fridge and joined her.

"You like?" he asked.

"Exactly what I would have ordered."

"How are you doing?"

She shrugged one shoulder and finished swallowing before she said, "I was in a holding pattern once. Flying back from New York to Miami from a conference. Damn, more than two hours waiting for a landing slot. Possibly worse, they showed a map of where we were in flight on the screen in front of us. It didn't help. But I also hadn't realized just how far one of those circles takes a plane. Dang, we could have landed at any number of major airports."

He snorted, still unwrapping his sandwich. "That would have made the passengers *so* happy."

"Might have been fun to watch the fireworks. Anyway, this is like a holding pattern, only it's not going to be over in a couple of hours."

"Nope."

"I got worried about the idea of someone in prison acting on Andy's directions."

Adam studied her, wishing she looked better, as

she had when he met her. Hardly to be wondered that stress was taking a toll on her.

She spoke again. "What did you tell Iris about why the sheriff was here?"

"Just that they were looking into some vandalism and wondered if I knew anything about it."

Jazz looked up. "You think she bought it?"

He shrugged. "That girl may think she's feeling better, and maybe she is a little, but not by that much. She didn't look any too steady going up those stairs."

"No, she didn't." Jazz sighed then ate another bite of her sandwich. "I should have told her she couldn't go upstairs because I'm not going to be her dumbwaiter."

He chuckled. "I didn't think of that. Well, I can ferry drinks and food up to her."

Jazz ate a little more. "I'm sure this tastes better than it seems to right now. Anyway, tomorrow I'm going back to some kind of normal. As in roasting that chicken I put in the fridge to thaw. Maybe even get some writing done. What about you?"

"I'm beginning to feel like a fifth wheel. Is my presence annoying you?" He braced himself.

She appeared startled. "No! Why would it? It's not like you're flopped on the couch demanding chips and dip and more beer."

"Still…" He needed to watch over these two, but he couldn't escape the possibility that he might be unwanted.

"Stop it," she said sharply. "You're helping. You're making me feel safer, especially about Iris. I'm sorry it's boring you to tears."

"It's not boring me at all, and I'd still have the same impatience and worry across the street. I'd be peering out the window round the clock and hoping nothing was going on in your backyard."

Sheba, who had quietly joined them to lie on the floor in her favorite corner, huffed. Adam looked at her immediately. He didn't hear that sound from her very often.

"Sheba? Is something wrong?"

The dog rose and stretched, then came over to the table, her tag jingling quietly. She sat and looked from one to the other.

"What is it, girl?"

A cocked head.

"Oh, crap," Adam said as he understood.

"What?"

He looked at Jazz. "I think she feels the pack broke up when Iris went upstairs. She wants us all together."

"Seriously?"

"Dogs can be like that." He returned his attention to the setter. "Go find Iris."

The dog took off like a shot and soon they heard the thud of her paws on the stairs.

Jazz laughed. "I guess you got that one right."

"I am not always stupid, although Sheba makes me feel like it sometimes."

He finished his sandwich, his mind running around like a hamster in a wheel, when finally he shook himself. *No.* This was a waste of time and energy.

"Let's get away from this damn table. There's got to be something on television. And Sheba will let us know if Iris needs something."

ANOTHER DAY DAWNED, once again chilly and rainy. Iris didn't even talk about going to school. "It's not that bad, Aunt Jazz, but I still don't feel good. Maybe by Monday?"

"I sure hope so, or I'm taking you to the doctor if I have to handcuff you."

"We'll see." Despite not feeling well, Iris managed to look stubborn.

"Ready to come downstairs and join the world for breakfast?"

"Yeah. But I'm not really hungry."

"You should eat a little unless you're sick to your stomach."

Jazz waited outside the bathroom while her niece took a shower. Iris changed into sloppy clothes that must make Lily shudder, but apparently Iris found them comfy. Socks on her feet, they headed downstairs.

Adam had beat Jazz to it. He was scrambling eggs with cheese and building a stack of buttered toast. "Sit down, ladies. This is one meal I can deal with."

Iris picked at her breakfast, but at least she ate.

Then she looked at the two of them. "When are you going to tell me what's going on?"

Adam and Jazz both froze. Then Jazz cleared her throat.

"What do you mean, Iris?"

Iris shrugged. "Adam didn't move over here because he needs an exterminator. Aunt Jazz, you didn't know Adam long enough to be romancing at that point. Then the sheriff shows up. I don't believe he came to question Adam about some vandalism. The top guy doesn't do that, he sends one of his deputies. So try another lie."

Jazz looked at Adam. Adam looked at Jazz. Flummoxed, Jazz then looked at her niece. She didn't want to lie, but upon reflection she had decided she didn't want Iris to live in fear. The threat was clearly directed at Lily, not her.

"A postcard," Adam said, filling the awkward silence. "It was addressed to Lily but sounded kind of threatening. I suppose we should check to see if there were any more in the mail."

Iris shook her head. "I'd have noticed a postcard. I had to throw away enough of those glossy ones. Did you know you can get a free dental exam? In Casper? Sheesh."

Jazz tried to smile and thought she felt her mouth respond to the urge.

Iris frowned though. "Do you think Mom's in danger?"

"I think," Jazz said, choosing her words with

care, "that we need to find out who this bully is so that your mom doesn't have to get cards like that when she gets home. But there might not ever be another one."

Iris seemed content with that. For now anyway. She ate a few more mouthfuls, then said, "I'm getting a headache. Can I have some ibuprofen?"

Jazz didn't see anything wrong with that. Adam beat her to the punch though, bringing the bottle to the table. "I'll join you. We can have a pill party."

Iris giggled at that. "But where's the beer?"

Adam arched his brows. "Have you looked at the clock?"

Another giggle from Iris. "You'd never let me have one. Mom wouldn't either, which is okay by me. It smells bad."

Jazz ate well, complimenting Adam on his scrambled eggs. "Light and fluffy. Not everyone can do that."

Iris spoke. "Can I go watch TV? Maybe cricket?"

A mere glance at Iris told Jazz the girl was looking worse again. "You really like it, huh?"

"Now that I understand better what's going on. T20 you called it?"

"Because there are only twenty overs, or 120 balls, in a game for each side. Fast."

"It seems like it."

They soon had Iris back in the recliner with a warm blanket and a can of chilled soda, which seemed a contradiction, but Jazz shrugged mentally, thinking, *Kids!*

She found a game on TV for Iris, warning her that it was a rerun and might be chopped up.

"That's okay. I like the highlights."

With Iris settled, Jazz and Adam returned to the kitchen table. Jazz decided she was going to hate that table, even though in her small studio at home she didn't have much better but she didn't spend as much time at it.

Sheba ran back and forth between the kitchen and the living room as if she couldn't decide where she wanted to be.

"Split pack?" Jazz asked.

"Maybe. Or she feels everyone needs her attention."

"That's entirely possible. Got any thoughts, Adam?"

"Yeah. This sucks. I guess we wait to see if there's another postcard."

"Or worse." Once again she was trying not to crawl out of her skin, trying to tell herself she was overreacting. "Don't you want to get back to your place? Back to your job?"

"Sometimes I go weeks without a broken water heater, backed up septic system, a leaking pipe, an oven that's not working, a blocked dryer vent. Amazing."

He made her want to laugh, and she decided to give in to it.

He smiled back. "Have you heard my cell phone quack?"

"Quack? Seriously?"

"It gets my attention." Dragging him away from places he didn't want to go, placing him firmly back in the present. He was all in favor of any trick that worked. The quack usually did, but not always.

The war haunted him, but it haunted many others. Like a dream, a repetitious nightmare that wouldn't go away. Except that it wasn't a nightmare. Sometimes it happened in the bright light of day. It was *real*.

Sometimes the past became the present, as real as the woman sitting at the table with him. Maybe things triggered him, but so far he hadn't found many of the triggers. If he had, he might have been able to avoid them.

Instead the memories hovered at the distant edge of consciousness and burst forth at the time of their choosing. He had to sit there and wonder if it would happen soon, happen in front of Jazz. The idea sickened him.

Not something he could afford to worry about. It was out of his control.

But hell, so was this maniac who was determined to frighten Lily. Maybe that's all he intended. Just to frighten her, but the squirrel really disturbed him. That took some kind of bent mind.

Just then, his phone quacked.

"Duty calls," Jazz remarked. She got up to get some coffee.

Adam answered his phone. "Hi Jess." Jess was rounding up the group for tonight. "Sorry, can't make the meeting tonight. See you next week, I hope. Yeah, okay. You, too."

She brought two cups to the table. "Meeting?"

"My vets group."

"You should go. You can't stay here *all* the time."

Annoyance rose in him. "Damn it, Jazz, if you want me out of here, just say so." Instantly he wished he could take the words back. The expression on her face, a mixture of shock and hurt and something else he couldn't identify.

"Don't take it that way," she said quietly. "I'm not giving you an eviction notice. I'm just concerned because you must have other things to do. Better things than babysitting me and Iris."

His irritation remained despite his regret for his outburst. "Listen, lady. I ain't got one better thing to do than make sure Iris and you are safe. Period."

She bit her lip and leaned back against the counter, forgoing her chair. "But it seems like such a small thing…"

"Really?" he asked harshly. *"Really?"*

After a few seconds, she shook her head. "No. It doesn't." She closed her eyes. "Those flowers felt like a death wish. The squirrel like a serious threat. The postcard would be nothing without those things."

"Exactly. Maybe it *is* all nothing. Maybe some creep is just getting his jollies. But what if he isn't? That's why you're so uneasy all the time. That's why you wish you didn't have to let Iris out of your sight. And I don't think you're overreacting. The only good thing I can say is that this doesn't seem to be in any way directed at your niece."

"There *is* that." At last she came to sit and reach for her coffee. The mug was still warm, and the coffee felt good going down her throat. Heat. She needed heat. Maybe she should go borrow one of Lily's heavier sweaters.

The kitchen window revealed a gray, drizzly day. Cold and damp, at least to her Florida blood.

Adam rose. "I'm going to take Sheba for a walk. Will you be okay for twenty minutes or so?"

It seemed strange to even be asked. "Of course."

Five minutes later, Adam and his dog were out the door. Jazz sat with her hands wrapped around her mug wondering if she would ever feel warm again. Or completely unafraid.

BY THE TIME Adam and Sheba returned, Jazz had moved to the living room and was watching cricket with Iris, who was eating crackers with liver sausage and cheese.

Content to see her niece eating a larger amount, Jazz explained the finer points of the game while Iris got involved enough to have developed a favorite team, at least in this match. She quietly cheered a good hit, groaned when someone lost a wicket, and had even started paying attention to the bowlers' styles. She was going to have mastered the game before the weekend was over.

Then her phone rang and she answered. "Oooh, school's out. Hi, Betsy! Yeah, I'm feeling a little better. Are you over it yet?"

School was out. Smiling, Jazz left Iris to her endless phone calls with friends and returned to the kitchen where Adam was wiping Sheba with a towel.

"I'm going to need to mop the floor," he remarked. "Sheba couldn't resist the puddles or the mud. Thank God she didn't roll around in it, but her paws!"

They were certainly muddy and had left prints all the way from the door. "Nothing that can't be fixed."

"This animal is going to tempt me to throw her in the bathtub."

But Sheba, oblivious to the threat, sat grinning and soaking up the rubdown.

"Let me get the dishpan," Jazz suggested. "You can save her the indignity of a bath."

"She'd love that," Adam agreed. "Despite how many she's had, she'll never like a bath."

Adam made Sheba sit while Jazz filled the dishpan with lukewarm water. "I don't want her running in to see Iris until she won't traipse mud everywhere."

Surprising Jazz, Sheba didn't seem to mind having her paws dipped in the water and gently rubbed by Adam. She lowered her nose a few times to sniff, then raised it, swiping Adam once with her tongue.

"I guess she likes that," Jazz remarked. She brought another towel so Adam could dry the dog's feet.

"She's an attention hog," Adam said fondly. When he was satisfied and sat back on his heels, Sheba ran in a few circles then raced to the living room.

"Zoomies," Adam remarked. He rose stiffly and picked up the wet towels.

"You cold and wet?" Jazz asked. Just then she heard Iris exclaim from the living room.

"Sheba! You never jump up!"

Adam waited, clearly listening, then Iris's giggle floated to them. No problem.

"I'm not too cold for a beer," Adam said, answering her question.

Jazz noticed he got himself some ibuprofen as well. Then he sagged onto a chair with a muffled curse. "Damp, cold weather."

"Makes you hurt worse?"

"I'm that old story about rheumatism making the knees ache. It'll pass. I should have asked if you want a beer."

"I know my way to the fridge. And soon I'm going to have to remember how to roast a chicken.

I used to do it all the time, but now I'm hazy on details."

"I'm sure the internet can help. It's saved my bacon more than once."

She retrieved her laptop and opened it, remarking, "I bet there's at least ten different recipes for it."

He snorted. "Pick the one that looks simplest. The way you *would* have made it before everybody's recipe was online."

Iris's giggles reached them as Jazz pored through web pages and the laughter had an odd effect on her. She looked across the table at Adam.

"I'm not afraid anymore," she announced.

"No?" He arched a brow.

"No. What I am is angry and getting angrier." Indeed, it was burning inside her like a coal fire, growing steadily. Fear was evaporating in a determination to stop this creep before he made her sister's life into a living hell. "You're right about this guy being a coward. That same kind of coward Andy was, picking on smaller and weaker people."

She felt stupid for not having thought of Andy from the beginning, but in her mind he was off the table while he was still in prison. Jazz, however, was sure of one thing: this crap would stir those memories in Lily, and God knew how her sister would handle them.

And what if Andy had somehow obtained an early release? God, she'd seen the guy in court, she'd listened to and watched the images and stories that Lily had told. She'd known her sister, for the first and only time in her life, on the edge of a nervous breakdown.

Stuck here, unable to identify the creep behind this, or to know what he might do next, infuriated her. Adam was right. She needed to keep impersonating Lily in the hope this snake would emerge from under his rock before Lily came home.

"What made you angry?" Adam asked.

"Thinking about Lily. I was afraid before like some kind of chicken but I'm afraid now for Lily. Given what she's been through with her ex, how do you imagine this might hit her? That creep she was married to nearly broke her. I never, ever, want to see that again."

"I can hardly imagine."

"You don't want to. But I was with her through the endgame, from the time the police arrested that man to his sentencing. The day he was sentenced was the first time I saw her smile in ages. A *real* smile. I'd die before I'd let her lose that smile."

Adam finished his beer, then got himself another one. Facing her again, he said, "Tell me about it."

"Tell you what?"

"About exactly what got Lily to that point. I don't understand the abuse dynamic. You told me generally, but I still don't fully get it."

Jazz sighed. "Most people don't. The first they want to know is why didn't she just leave. I think I told you."

"But she didn't. From what I've seen of her, and you, it leads me to believe it's far from that simple."

"It is. Books helped me better understand, but it's basically simple. Lovebirds. Seemingly solid relationship. Eventual separation from friends and family because the guy just doesn't like them. Because he gets irritated when she sees them. Alongside this is steadily increasing abuse. At first he always apologizes. Brings flowers or gifts and swears he'll never do it again. He lets her know in no uncertain terms that he wouldn't have gotten mad except for something she said or did. So then she tries harder to become the perfect wife."

"God," Adam muttered.

"Natural reaction to want to make the person you love happy. But then it moves past that to *fear* of making him angry. And because you've distanced yourself from everyone you could trust, you're all alone with this guy. He's your only support. Or so you believe. From there the abuse just ratchets up, and because of your fear of him you'll lie even when he sends you to the hospital."

She heard Adam nearly growl.

"So, into this comes Iris, a baby he didn't want and got stuck with anyway. And Iris becomes his cudgel. Threats against her if Lily doesn't behave."

He swore forcefully. "Then the bastard hurt Iris."

"Yeah. That yanked Lily out of the whole cycle. Sliced through her fear of him and her fear of failing him." She paused and closed her eyes briefly.

"Sometimes, for some people, that's not enough to make them get out. The terror is overwhelming, the feeling of no escape is controlling."

"But there are safe houses, aren't there?"

"Sure. But a lot a victims can no longer believe in safety. Often for good reason. He'll find them, they're sure."

Adam wiped one hand over his face. "What an ugly, ugly picture."

Jazz looked down. "Imagine living with the guilt afterward. The shame. Anyway, counseling seemed to help them both, like I said, and Lily picked up her career and made huge strides from the place where Andy had kept her stuck. But I don't want this to take her back there. No way. We've got to prevent that."

"I can't agree more. But we're stymied now. We need him to make a mistake."

She nodded. "At least this creep doesn't seem interested in Iris." As soon as she spoke the words, a shiver ran down her spine.

Not Iris. But how could they be sure?

Dread filled her. A dark, deep dread.

ANDY HAD DEVELOPED a well of patience in prison, but that well wasn't very deep. He was reaching the bottom of it now and he could barely stand the waiting any longer.

He decided it might be a good time to return to

Conard City. Just for a look around. A way to plan what he wanted to do, not just think about it.

Imagining it had been good enough during nearly ten years in prison. It had carried him through the rocky weeks after his early discharge. He'd left that damn prison without anything except the clothes and wallet he'd arrived with. Essentially no money at all.

But he'd managed anyway. A day labor job here and there, money good enough for a man who was now used to nearly nothing. Even meals were better at homeless shelters than at the prison.

Dumpster diving had become his friend. Hitchhiking worked if he avoided cops.

But now he needed to be in total control of his journey. Control was massively important to him. He hadn't had any for years now.

He hungered for it, and that bitch had stolen every bit of control he'd had. He wanted it back. All of it. Most especially of Lily. He'd never forgotten how he'd savored treating her like a dog and having her scramble to follow his every command.

That beautiful, supposedly powerful, woman had held no power when it came to him. He'd held it all.

Hell, except for her job that supported him, he'd have dressed her in rags just to prove his point.

Time to get going, he decided. He needed to smell her fear again, to see it in her eyes, and playing his little games wasn't enough. While he enjoyed the idea of her receiving his most recent postcard, it didn't satisfy him. Yeah, he was edging her back into a pliable state, but maybe he could find a faster way to do it.

His financial situation, as he thought of it, didn't allow him to get a car, so late at night he borrowed one from a used car lot just beyond the outskirts of Laramie. Then he helped himself to plates from a truck elsewhere in town. He mailed one last postcard from there, checked his money and the credit card he'd heisted from a guy's wallet in Casper, and left town.

The credit card would work for a tank of gas, but not much beyond that, he figured. He chose to head east for gas when Conard County was west. Muddying his trail. He wasn't stupid.

Then he would set out for Conard County. He'd been away for a few days, and nobody had seemed interested in him when he was there. This time he'd stay farther away. Maybe keep this well-used pickup mostly out of sight.

Maybe heist an ATV somewhere along the way. You never knew, but it was good to plan for possibilities.

Smiling, he gassed the truck then turned toward Conard City. Oh, this was going to be good.

*Chapter Twelve*

Monday morning brought cheerier weather, and Iris headed back to school with one caveat from Jazz.

"Take it easy with the swimming today. You don't want to make yourself sick again."

Iris breezed off, smiling happily, and Adam looked at Jazz.

"You think she'll listen?" he asked.

"No, but I had to say it."

He laughed. "What about you? Anything you'd like to do today?"

Well, she didn't have to worry about Iris while she was in school and with her friends. "Get out of this house. Take a walk in the fresh air. Maybe go to the grocery."

"That chicken you made was pretty good."

Jazz smiled. "I managed okay. Now I want to try something else. I've given up on writing until I get home."

"Do you feel bad about it?"

"My editor will probably feel worse. I think I'm

already scheduled for publication. Regardless, life happens, and it's happening right now. In ways I don't like." She shook herself. "No use thinking about that now. I'll wait until it's time for the mail. Then I can get uptight wondering if there's another postcard. Or worse."

Adam studied her, then spoke. "If you don't mind, I'll walk with you."

"I'd like that." Very much. Maybe too much. But what was the point? Much as she liked Adam, as attractive as she found him, she'd be going back to Miami.

But some nights in bed, when she could shake her worries, she thought about him. Lasciviously. Sometimes she even ached to know what it would be like to make love with him.

Egad, this was going nowhere except into trouble. And she had enough trouble right now.

"Then," he said, unaware of her thoughts and continuing the conversation, "I want to go over to my place and bring over some of my workout equipment. Maybe some weights and a mat. I'll put them in the basement."

Once again, guilt struck her. "I'm messing up your life."

"*You're* not messing up anything, and I'm doing exactly what I want to, okay? Now get your jacket. I'd call it spring out there, but you'd probably call it winter."

That called a needed laugh out of her. She hurried to get her lightweight jacket and joined him on the porch.

"The coast is clear," he said in a conspiratorial voice.

She had to grin. "You're good for me," she announced.

"Ditto."

They climbed down the porch steps then stood on the sidewalk. "Which way?" Adam asked.

"The prettiest route to the grocery."

He led her a few blocks over to a wider avenue. The leaves were new, the light green that came before the darker color of summer. Still a little feathery in places. Branches overhung the street, making it almost tunnel-like except for the dappled sun that spilled through.

Large gracious houses lined the street on both sides, ornamented with Victorian gingerbread, boasting wide, deep front porches. Some even featured hanging bench swings; many were decorated with window boxes, flowers just beginning to bloom.

"This place is enchanted," Jazz said.

"Another era." He pointed to a gray-painted clapboard house with darker gray trim. "Sheriff Dalton lives there with his wife, the librarian. Miss Emma."

She tilted her face toward him. "Miss Emma? Really?"

"Seems outdated, doesn't it? But evidently she's been called that since she became librarian in her early twenties. No one seems to know why. Maybe it was kids being taught to be respectful back then. Regardless, she'll always be Miss Emma."

"I like that."

"Well, that's her family house. Her father was Judge Conard, and the Conards were one of the founding families here. As if the name wouldn't tell you. Word is that she's collected the history of this area going back as far as possible. And, I hear, she's still collecting stuff. There's no escape from history around here. Best behave."

Jazz laughed again. The world was lightening, for however long it might last, and she was happy to take the gift.

She felt bad when she realized Adam's limp had grown more obvious, but he didn't say anything and she kept her mouth shut. It must be awful living with continuous pain but it wasn't her place to draw attention to his limp unless he said something. They continued their circuitous route to the store through residential streets.

ADAM'S HIP WAS killing him, more than usual. He wanted to suppress his pain but couldn't. And he didn't want to see pity in Jazz's eyes.

She kept on drawing him the way Lily never had, even though they looked as if they'd sprung from the same mold. Both were confident women, successful in their careers. Lily had never appeared to be interested in men anyway, and now he understood why. He simply couldn't imagine the hell she'd lived through.

Maybe that was the difference he sensed. At times he thought he caught a spark of sexual interest in Jazz's gaze, but then it flitted away.

Naturally it would. She would be leaving in a few weeks, going back to her own life and friends. Besides, what would she want with a battered vet who still struggled with PTSD?

Anyway, they both had more important things to think about, like the threat to Lily. Given Lily's background, he agreed with the need to put this all to bed before she returned.

At the grocery, Jazz mulled over the available food. She appeared to be considering what she might cook that night. There had to be at least one recipe in her head the way she was looking around. Or maybe she was mentally assembling one.

After a bit, she'd filled her cart. "Okay," he said, "what's the menu?"

"Fruit for Iris of course. I believe she keeps an entire fruit farm in business. Apples, oranges, bananas. Orange juice. Gads, she doesn't have to worry about sugar, either. I'm totally envious of that girl."

He laughed.

"Cereal. Oats. Crackers, whole wheat. Bread, multigrain. She'll settle for rye, though."

"Okay, okay, I get it."

"Well, she *did* ask if I thought she could eat that

delicious meal you brought home from the diner. French fries? Never will they pass her lips."

"I think I saw her snag a couple."

"I never saw. She's safe."

Now he was grinning.

"And the rest of the stuff?" The ingredients were making little sense to him except for the lasagna noodles and jar of high-class marinara. Cheese, a few pounds of hamburger.

"I'll make meatloaf tonight. Lasagna tomorrow when I have more time."

"Ambitious." Meatloaf? He hated it.

She cocked an eye at him as she added golden mushroom soup and A-1 sauce to the cart. "I know what you're thinking. Meatloaf is dry." She winked. "Mine is not. In fact, it's famous with my friends."

"Okay. Just don't say tuna casserole."

"Maybe I'll make tuna salad one of these days."

"Now that I like. In fact, I'll make it."

"I may definitely put you on it."

As she checked out, he looked at the growing stack of groceries. The bagger, however, was packing the bags pretty full. "I should have brought my truck. It's a good thing we can carry all this between us."

She smiled. A sweet expression always. He'd like to keep it on her face. "I was counting on you."

He took the heaviest doubled bags, leaving her the lighter ones. He knew for sure he had the muscle strength.

The walk home was good, despite his hip. He just enjoyed Jazz's company.

Back at the house he helped her unload everything. When he started to put away the soda crackers, onions and A-1 sauce, she said, "Not those."

"Really?"

"I put all my ingredients in my cooking space so I don't forget something or have to run around looking for it."

He nodded. "Good idea."

"You may get the dishwashing detail as I prepare, though."

"Not a problem, lady. I'm really experienced at that. I'm going to run across the street to bring some of my workout equipment over and put it in the basement, if you're okay with that."

He saw the fear return briefly to her gaze, but she said nothing except, "Go get it."

ADAM LIMITED HIMSELF to dumbbells and the exercise mat. He could do a lot on that mat to keep himself going for a while. He put it all in the basement. He returned to the top of the stairs in time to hear Iris come home. Early.

Then he heard the door bang. He looked in that direction, discovering this was no breezy, happy Iris. Instead she threw today's mail at the hall table, knocking the carefully stacked letters onto the floor.

"Sorry," she said pettishly, then stomped into the living room.

Adam turned a bit and saw Jazz in the kitchen doorway. "What's going on?"

"I guess I need to find out. I've never seen her in this mood."

"At her age she ought to be having more of them."

He remained in the hallway so he could eavesdrop, even though he knew he shouldn't. Still, he was concerned about Iris. If she had moods like this, he'd certainly never seen them or heard about them.

Jazz spoke gently. "What's wrong, Iris?"

"Sally!"

Silence. Adam waited, knowing that Sally was Iris's best friend. Now his curiosity was truly piqued.

"What about Sally?" Jazz asked.

"She stole my boyfriend! My best friend stole my boyfriend! I'm not going to swim today. Maybe never again 'cuz she's on the team!"

"Wow," Jazz said.

*Wow,* Adam thought.

"I didn't know you had a boyfriend. You said you didn't have time for one."

"It was mostly at school and we talked a lot on the phone at night. We even made plans for the summer. But he was holding hands with Sally today, and neither of them would look at me. So I asked her. Yeah, she stole him! She even knew about him and me, but she went ahead and did it anyway. And he's been calling her for a while. She didn't even tell me. He didn't tell me."

"That's pretty awful," Jazz said sympathetically.

What sounded like a sob issued from the living room. "I'm quitting the swim team."

"Because of Sally?"

"Because I don't ever want to see her again. Because I don't have time to go anywhere after school. The most I could do was a movie on the weekend, but we never did that. Homework! But Sally doesn't have any more time than I do, so it can't be that." Another sob. "He didn't like me as much as he said he did!"

"That's terrible." Jazz fell silent for a brief time. Then she said, "You probably don't want my opinion but you might want to look at this another way."

"There is no other way!"

"Yes," Jazz said firmly. "There is. Think about it. He didn't break up with you before he went wandering. Who needs a guy like that? What if he came back to you? Could you ever trust him?"

Iris sniffled for a while. "Maybe not."

"Basically, he cheated on you. And Sally has snagged a guy who is cheater."

More sniffling. "I should pick up the mail." Clearly trying to change the subject.

"I'll do it." Again Jazz fell silent for a minute or so. "You probably don't want to hear this, but here goes. Go to the swim practice tomorrow and act like you don't care. It won't be easy, but you'll keep your pride."

Iris sniffled again. "Maybe. Darn it, Aunt Jazz, you've got a whole different idea about this."

"Maybe because I've walked in your shoes. Just make yourself look like the better person. Of course, you don't have to listen to me. All your decision."

Adam heard Jazz stir, then she came out of the living room. He guessed she knew he'd been eavesdropping by the way she gave him a crooked smile.

"I'll pick up the mail," he offered.

"Leave it. It's a good comment on this day. Let's go make meatloaf."

Suddenly Iris's voice reached them, still sounding like she was on the edge of tears. "Not meatloaf! You've got be kidding!"

"Mine is famous," Jazz called back. "It's better than most."

In the kitchen, Adam headed straight to the fridge and pulled out a longneck. "Want one?"

"What I need is a stiff bourbon. But yes please."

They sat at the table, which seemed to have become their favorite gathering place.

"Like some help with that meatloaf?" he asked, not wanting to discuss the issue at hand for fear Iris might hear.

"What I want to do is dress down Sally and this boyfriend in a way they'll never forget. But that won't do any good at all and it would only embarrass Iris."

"An urge to violence." He smiled crookedly. He

liked her fire. Good to see it. Talk about getting overwhelmed on a simple visit to her niece. But he also felt a great deal of sympathy for Iris. Being scorned like that seriously hurt.

"Sucks," he said.

"More than sucks. It's hurtful. Agonizingly hurtful at that age. And humiliating."

"That, too. So, the meatloaf?"

"Just finish that beer and go do your workout. *I* want to take out my anger on the damn hamburger. I suppose the workout makes you feel better."

"In more than one way," he confessed. "It's a great way to deal with memories I don't want."

She tilted her head. "The war?"

"Yup." He turned his bottle up and drained it.

"And how's your hip after that walk to the grocery?"

"Grinding along as usual."

"Grinding?"

"No better way to describe it." But that was more than he wanted to say. "I'll go do the workout. You need anything at all, holler down the stairs."

"I will."

He detested the look of sympathy on her face. He didn't need sympathy. Not even a little of it. Should have kept his mouth shut.

He rinsed the bottle and threw it in the trash before limping toward the basement stairs. "I won't be long."

"Don't hurry on my account. That hamburger is going to get it."

He nearly chuckled. "Beat it to death." Then he climbed down the stairs.

DINNER WAS A subdued affair. Iris insisted on cleaning off half the dining room table and setting it. Then she said, "I'll pick up that mail. My fault."

"Leave it," said Jazz. "It suits my mood."

Iris struggled for a red-eyed smile. "Mine too, honestly. I hate to say it, but that meatloaf smells good."

"Oh, wonder of wonders. I told you it was famous. I'll make some broccoli and mashed potatoes in a little while. I should have baked a cake but your mom doesn't keep any boxed mixes around and it's the only kind I know how to make."

"I couldn't eat it anyway."

"Screw your training diet. I wouldn't mind if you broke it out of frustration anyway. You need chocolate but that's one other thing I don't have. I wasn't planning on a breakup."

Iris sniffled. "Neither was I, but next time I'll plan better."

"Keep a quart of chocolate ice cream at the back of the freezer for emergencies. Not that you'll probably have another one like this."

"Damn," said Iris. "I should have guessed. He's a jock."

"And you aren't?"

Another weak smile from the girl. But that was the end of her attempt to be sociable, and Jazz went to work on side dishes. The meatloaf was approaching done.

THEY SAT AT the table with Blue Willow plates, sliced meatloaf and sides. Each of them served themselves, Adam heaping his plate.

"Dang, this is a fantastic meatloaf," Adam said after tasting it. "I can see why it's famous."

Iris, who had been slowly forking it, finally tried a mouthful. Her eyes widened. "You weren't kidding. Okay I'll eat this again. But only yours."

Then conversation lagged. Iris ate with heavy sighs, and Adam and Jazz were both disinclined to converse in the face of all that misery.

After dinner, Iris wanted to do the dishes and Jazz insisted on helping her.

Girl time, Adam thought. He left them to it and went to the hallway to clean up the spilled mail. It might suit Jazz's mood to leave it, but he had a concern: another postcard. Maybe that was why Jazz didn't want Iris to straighten up the mess, and maybe she wanted the mess left because she feared what she might find.

So he bent to the task, lifting and stacking until he uncovered a post card.

*I'm coming and you'll never know when.*

Adam's heart slammed, then rage filled him. Another threat, this one stronger. He tucked the card inside his shirt pocket. He didn't want to show it to Jazz, but it would be wrong to keep her in the dark. She had a right to know and she wasn't a child.

He started stacking the remaining mail when he saw an official envelope. "Holy Mary," he murmured. "Damn it all."

He looked up, staring into space, then straightened and put the envelope under others to conceal it. He decided to place the postcard there as well. After Iris went up for the night, he'd talk with Jazz.

## Chapter Thirteen

Andy arrived in Conard County that same night. He parked his stolen truck out of sight under some low-hanging trees in the middle of nowhere.

He'd snagged a sleeping bag earlier from an empty tent in a rustic campground, and when he'd bought gas on the credit card—which would soon be smoking hot—he'd picked up enough food and beer to keep him going for days. The bed of the truck, with its camper shell, made a perfect bedroom and dining room for him.

Tomorrow he'd go looking for Lily and an opportunity. Although he was beginning to think Iris might provide that opportunity. He'd spotted his daughter on his last visit to this ink spot town and had felt slammed. He identified her easily because she was almost a carbon copy of Lily except for that hair.

Talk about getting even! To torture Lily once again with their kid. Yeah, he liked the symmetry of that.

Pleased with himself, he ate a stale turkey sandwich and a larger bag of potato chips.

Not that he'd ever hurt the kid. No, that was the single time he'd lost control. He was sure he could control himself when he needed to. Anger didn't rule him, and he was all about control.

What he never realized was that he'd never controlled himself to any meaningful extent except in prison. There, punishment and retribution came swiftly.

He'd never realized that his love of control was about controlling everyone except himself.

He listened to the murmur of the trees above, feeling very satisfied with himself.

IRIS WENT UPSTAIRS at her usual time, maybe to talk to girlfriends. Except for Sally.

Jazz had moved into the living room with Adam. "Good workout?" she asked. "And the hip?"

"I took more ibuprofen." He rose. "I know it's late, but I need a cup of coffee. You?"

She hesitated. "Something's going on. Tell me."

"When we've both got coffee. We're going to want to talk for a while, not sleep."

"Oh, God," she said quietly. "Another postcard?"

"In a minute, Jazz. In a minute."

He went to the kitchen to make coffee, leaving her nearly on the edge of her seat with anxiety. She'd never been a nail chewer, but she was considering it just then. Her fingers dug into the arms of the recliner. She knew something awful was coming just by the way he wasn't tossing out information.

Adam brought her coffee.

"All right," he said. "Well, it's not all right, but wait while I get the necessary mail."

"A postcard," she murmured, her mind rebelling, her anger returning. Whoever this was, he was playing cat and mouse with her and her sister. An ugly game to anyone who'd ever seen a cat play with a mouse. For a cat, it was a matter of survival, and the play wearied the prey until it would no longer retaliate. Which didn't make it any prettier. This guy was no cat but he seemed to be trying to tire his prey.

Adam returned with a postcard and an envelope. He sat while she scanned the postcard. Her stomach clenched into a painful knot.

"Dear God!" She tried to keep her voice low because of Iris, although she probably wouldn't hear anything except the friend's voice on the other end of her phone. "Dear God."

"Exactly. And this. It appears to have been in the stack since shortly after you arrived. No reason for Iris to pick it out."

This time her stomach flipped and nausea filled it. "No, she's observing her mother's privacy."

But written in hard black ink in the upper left-hand corner were the terrifying words:

*State of Florida.*

*Department of Corrections.*

"Adam..."

"Open it."

She lifted her head slowly, looking at him. "But it's addressed to Lily."

"Do you really think she'd complain to the post office that you opened her mail? Especially *that* mail?"

He was right, but she honestly didn't want to open it. She was positive it couldn't contain good news, such as that Andy had been shivved by another prisoner. Or that his sentence had been extended by ten years for some other misdeed.

She reluctantly, slowly, opened the top of the envelope, then pulled out the one-page letter. Her rollercoaster took another dive then rose to the height of fury.

"It's him," she said, her voice tight. "It's him." Then she passed the letter to Adam.

Adam scanned the page quickly. "I figured."

Andy Robins had been released early from prison on gain time. Something that almost never happened, not in Florida.

FOR A WHILE there didn't seem to be anything to say. Adam hated that he had no comfort to offer Jazz. Her eyes had gone almost hollow, but fury flared in their depths.

"We'll deal with it somehow," he said eventually. "We'll deal together. You're not alone."

The faintest smile whispered across her face. "Thanks."

"No need. Now let's go to our favorite perch in the kitchen and have a beer or more coffee." The beverage in their cups had grown cold. "I wish I'd dashed out earlier and gotten you some bourbon."

"Beer is fine. Maybe it'll help peel me off the ceiling."

"The ceiling isn't my favorite hangout," he agreed. Rising, he offered his hand to help her up.

She gripped him tightly, more tightly than necessary. He didn't mind, but it gave him a sense of her emotional state, more than anything she'd said.

In the kitchen, she dumped her coffee in the sink and left the cup on the counter, indicating she'd rather have a beer. He put his cup beside hers and switched off the pot. Focusing on ordinary tasks while his mind absorbed the enormity of this latest installment of *Terrifying Lily*. A horror show.

Yeah, he'd suspected this. Jazz probably had, too. The difference was that she had a very clear idea of what Andy Robbins could do. He was now no amorphous sleaze who'd just be content to spark fear. This was a man capable of serious violence.

Why couldn't the bastard have just gone elsewhere? Why this need to make Lily's life into a living hell?

Adam got the beers, glad he'd bought another six-pack at the store earlier. Had that been today? He was familiar from war with the way time could stretch, how mornings could seem so far in the past that they felt like another day. He just hadn't realized this was going to turn into one of *those* days.

Now it had.

He joined Jazz at the table, opening the longneck for her. Then he opened his own. The minutiae of detail seemed important now. Something to focus on besides the murderous fury inside himself.

Something to focus on besides the wish that he could sweep away this entire problem to make all the ladies safe. At least Iris had so far been sheltered from this, but could that continue?

When he thought of that innocent girl, his rage ramped up even more. She didn't need the trauma, the knowledge that someone wanted to hurt her mother. Memories of what her father had done to her had probably faded, maybe even been forgotten the way traumas sometimes were, as if the mind could wall them off. Plus she'd been so young.

He had to protect Iris from all of that.

But how? His hand tightened around the cold bottle he held. For him, the worst of this was not knowing exactly how this guy would carry through. How far he would go. How to stop him if he couldn't be found. How he could put an end to this.

Not being able to plan except in the most general way.

Jazz spoke. "I'll get a gun," she said. "A shotgun because I won't need much of an aim. If that bastard shows up anywhere near this house, I'll kill him and I don't care if I spend the rest of my life in prison."

He didn't tell her how killing a person, even a person who was threatening you, could haunt your days and nights forever. Why bother? He was prepared to do the same, and he was already haunted by faces he would never forget. By the internal graveyard he carried.

"I'll teach you how to use it," he said. And he would. Everyone deserved self-defense. "He's a cockroach."

"A snake."

"Aww, don't get hard on snakes. They only act against us in self-defense."

Jazz's face had hardened until it was unreadable, then the faintest of smiles flickered over her lips. "You're right. He's *human*."

"Kind of the worst of it. I heard somewhere that out of all our primate cousins, the only ones who fight wars and kill each other are chimpanzees. I don't think we've improved much."

She sighed, finally drinking some beer and letting her face relax. "I'm not going to sleep tonight."

"Me neither. Maybe we'll catch a few Z's tomorrow while Iris is safe at school."

"How am I going to let her racket around by herself?"

"I don't think she's ever alone, Jazz. The guy's after Lily, but even so if he tried to snatch Iris her friends would raise hell, too. Not an easy nab."

"No." Again she sighed. "Damn it, Adam. Damn it. That monster deserved more than he got, and he should still be in prison. Hell, he should have been sent up for life."

Adam frowned. "Didn't they charge him with multiple crimes?"

"You bet. I don't remember them all. What I *do* remember was the judge running the sentences concurrently instead of stacking them. He could have done that. I'm not one to think people ought to spend all their lives in prison, but when they're violent like that? Over the span of years? Does anyone really expect them to learn a lesson?"

"Lily's ex probably didn't. If this is her ex. No way to be sure, but the timing is suspicious."

"Oh, it's Andy all right. Lily was terrified of him for good reason."

Adam drank more beer. Nearly ready for a second. "You know, I never would have guessed that Lily had been through such a hell. Nothing about her suggests it."

"She's overcome it, but I think she's putting on a brave face sometimes." Jazz rested her chin in her hand. "What a nightmare. I'm so glad Lily isn't here."

So was he, but he was wishing Jazz wasn't here either. Nor Iris. But how would that help? The creep would find another time to do this, assuming it *was* Lily's ex.

He reached across the table and covered Jazz's free hand with his own. Her bones felt so small and delicate. All of her appeared delicate. "Go lie down, Jazz. I'm here."

"Lie down and be all alone with my imagination? I don't think so."

"You don't have to be alone."

He heard her draw a sharp breath. He hadn't meant that the way she was probably taking it, but he didn't rephrase himself. Instead he stood up. "Come on. You can lie down and I'll be nearby. Talk if you need to. But if you don't get out of that damn chair your butt is going to hurt and you're going to freeze in that position."

He persuaded her to stretch out on her bed. She removed her shoes, her only concession, and covered herself with a blue Sherpa throw.

"Oh, for Pete's sake," she said irritably as he sat in the corner chair. "Lie down, too. You must need to stretch some."

So he did, but he left his boots on, and he didn't need a blanket to keep him warm. Being near Jazz was doing a good enough job of that.

DESPITE HERSELF, JAZZ fell into a restless slumber. When eventually she stirred, it was still dark outside but she hardly noticed.

Sometime while she slept, she had become wrapped in Adam's arms. She knew she had crawled into them because she had moved away from the edge of the bed toward him.

His embrace was welcoming, holding her close, a hug that felt so good she wanted it never to stop.

Daringly, she snuggled in a little closer and felt

his arms tighten. God, she ached for this comfort. Ached for him.

Then, to her embarrassment, she realized he was awake. "I'm sorry," she said, her voice still cracking from sleep.

"For what?"

"Umm, for crowding you?"

"You haven't. We both needed some relaxation and I guess we got it."

She pulled away, still embarrassed, but with anxiety beginning to creep in again. She sat up and yawned, hating how much she missed his arms. She had to remind herself once again that she was going back to Miami. "I need a shower."

He stood up. "Take it. I'll meet you in our favorite kitchen."

The shower eased some of the tension from her and she was tempted to remain longer, but remembering that Iris would probably need some hot water soon, she made sure to leave some.

Fresh clothes felt good, too, making her feel almost like her old self. Since arriving here, she *had* become a new woman, a changed woman. Ugliness was touching her in ways it seldom did.

Tempting smells were emerging from the kitchen. With her hair wrapped in a towel and her shoulders wrapped in Lily's wooly burgundy shawl, she stepped into the room to find Adam at the stove.

"Bacon," he said. "To be followed by toast and

eggs. I make a mean scrambled egg as I'm sure you've noticed. Coffee's ready."

"Anything I can do?"

"Grab a cup and take a seat. I don't work well with others."

A snort escaped her. "I *so* believe that."

A sound from above caught Jazz's attention. "Iris is waking up."

"I made enough bacon for her, too, but I bet she doesn't eat it. Toast and eggs though, maybe."

"She hasn't exactly been following her training diet the last few days."

"I wouldn't always either, without a multimillion-dollar contract."

Casual conversation that was helping the morning feel normal. Except it wasn't normal.

She spoke to Adam's back as he stood at the stove. "You always live here?"

"Born and raised. My dad was a hired hand out at the Stiller spread. Then he got too old to work, my mom died of heart failure and Dad killed himself."

"Oh my God! I'm so sorry, Adam."

He turned to place a platter of bacon on the counter nearby. "They had a decent life. It wasn't easy but as far as I know they were happy. I'm sure of one thing. My dad wouldn't have offed himself if he'd been able to live without my mother."

"Hard on you, though."

"I was in the Army by then, kinda focused on my own survival. It hurt, sure, but it took a while for it to sink in. And by then the grief had already softened. How many eggs?"

"Two please." She felt ravenous.

"I'll make two for Iris. So seven eggs."

There went most of the carton. Not that Jazz minded. She simply added it to her mental list for the next trip to the grocery. And there *would* be another trip out, she vowed. Staying in this house all the time would drive her crazy.

But when Iris was safely at school, why not leave the house unattended…as long as Adam was willing to come with her.

Going out alone didn't seem like a smart thing to do right now.

Iris appeared, hair a bit damp. She evidently still hadn't recovered from her betrayal by Sally and the "boyfriend." Not that she was likely to anytime soon. Life's hard knocks hurt.

Iris hesitated over the bacon, then took two strips along with her plate of eggs and four pieces of toast.

"Swimming today?" Jazz asked.

Iris's expression became determined. "You bet. I'll show them I don't give a gosh darn."

Adam spoke. "Way to go."

ANDY ROBBINS WATCHED Iris emerge from the house with her school backpack and a small duffel. He'd already learned that she swam every day from the guy at the gas station who was only too willing to talk when Andy said he knew Lily from college. Today he'd follow her to discover her route and if she'd ever be alone.

Iris would be the best tool to get at Lily, he had decided. The very best. Either way, with Lily or Iris, he'd use the chloroform he'd made.

Amazing what you could learn how to do in prison.

Satisfied with his decision, he needed only to figure out what he'd do with one or both of them, depending. If Iris became his lever against Lily, he might have to handle this a whole different way.

Digesting all this, he headed back to his campsite with a few items from the convenience store at the gas station. Wonder of wonders, the credit card still worked, but he should find another one soon before this one blew up in his face.

Another problem to consider. He sure didn't want to draw attention in this town.

He cooked himself a little Spam over a small fire and downed it with beer.

Lily must be afraid by now. He considered all he had done so far and nodded approvingly. It could be anyone who'd done those things.

She'd probably have heard from the Department of Corrections that he was out now, too.

But she'd never, ever, think that after all these years he would follow her over this huge distance. Nope.

Lily had never been *that* bright.

IRIS TRUDGED TO swim practice alone. Once she had walked this way with Sally, but no more. Never again.

But she was going to have her revenge by acting as if she didn't care at all. Aunt Jazz was right about that.

She barely noticed the creaky old pickup that drove past. Plenty of those around here. Plenty.

Instead she focused on the wild land that filled the road on both sides. The college still hadn't reached out and gobbled it all up. Better for the environment if they didn't. Besides, she loved the wildflowers, a few hardy ones blossoming despite the cold weather they'd had a few times this spring.

She loved it here, but she still hoped she wouldn't be around to see that land developed. She'd lived here long enough to know this place was on a boom and bust cycle through the years. It was in a bust cycle now, but that would change.

Things always changed.

ADAM WENT TO do his workout midafternoon. The basement was dark but illuminated well enough by overhead bulbs that he could manage his equipment. The long fluorescent light above the washer and dryer added to the fight against darkness.

The space was occupied, of course, by the washer and dryer, as well as the water heater and the furnace, but all of that left him plenty of room.

When he'd worked as many muscles as he could

without some of his equipment, he headed upstairs, pleasantly sweaty. A shower next, if Jazz was okay.

Boy, had she stepped into a mess when she agreed to watch Iris. It had probably sounded like an easy job and it would have been except for some creep with ugly things on his mind.

Now this breakup. Adam really felt sorry for the girl and she was too young yet to believe that someone better would come along. In the days ahead, she'd get past this betrayal. Because it *had* been a betrayal, the kind that tended to leave scars.

He would know. He'd had a relationship like that. Cindy Lou Brown. Big mistake, but it would have been easier if he hadn't discovered her cheating. Lots of cheating. No one man was good enough for Cindy Lou.

But she sure did like presents, especially expensive ones.

He shook off the memory and looked for Jazz, finding her in that little office room to the back.

"Working?" he asked.

"Trying to."

"Mind if I go take a shower?"

She swiveled her chair around. "Now why would I mind?"

"Oh, I can think of a reason or two. I'm off, back shortly."

She turned back to her laptop and he headed upstairs, wondering if he'd interrupted her work. Maybe he should just leave her alone when she was staring at that machine. Not say a word, rude as it would feel.

He still needed to tell Gage Dalton about that letter. Maybe Gage could dredge up a mug shot of Lily's ex and give it out to his deputies. That would make both him and Jazz feel better. Marginally.

Hot showers were a luxury he still enjoyed fully. Years in the Army had exposed him to enough cold showers to last a lifetime.

His hip had begun to shriek again, so the next thing on his list was that ibuprofen bottle. He toweled off quickly, dressed just as quickly in a flannel shirt and jeans, then headed downstairs on a hip that wondered if it should support his weight.

God, he hated it when it got like this. Pain was one thing, weakness another.

When he reached the foot of the stairs, Jazz came out of the office. "I give up!" she said.

"Did I break your concentration?"

"As if I had any." She marched toward the kitchen. "I thought escaping into my fantasy world would make me feel better. It usually does. I'm beginning to think nothing will make me feel better until we get rid of this creep, and I don't care anymore *how* we do it. He needs to be erased just for all this anxiety and aggravation."

Wow, that was a statement, coming from Jazz. "Did you call the sheriff about that letter?"

"What good will that do?"

"Maybe he can pull up this guy's mug shot. Share it with all the cops."

She paused just as she reached the coffee maker. "I didn't think of that."

"I didn't exactly hop all over it, either."

"We're getting too tired and worn out. Which is why I'm making more coffee. I may never want to see any caffeine again after this."

"I wouldn't blame you." He grabbed the ibuprofen and swallowed them dry before easing into the chair. Well, that didn't help.

"Pain again?" she asked.

"There's no *again* about it."

She sighed, looking sad, but didn't speak. She headed for the pantry.

When she did speak, it was to say, "God knows what I'm going to make for dinner tonight."

"Let me take a peek."

"You stay in that chair until the ibuprofen hits. There's got to be something in here that I recognize."

He could have laughed if they weren't both feeling so unhappy and edgy.

"Well, I found some granola bars, Adam. Want a couple?"

"Please."

She emerged holding the box in her hand, then placed it in front of him. "I'll have one, too, while I try to figure out dinner."

That sent her straight to the freezer. "Fish. More

fish. I should have succumbed and bought a beef roast. Or another chicken. Or some pork chops."

"I have some pork chops at my place. Let me run over and get them. It's one thing I cook often enough."

She smiled faintly. "That would be nice."

So he hiked himself out before the coffee was ready, before he ate one of the granola bars. He returned a few minutes later with frozen chops and a six-pack.

Jazz eyed the beer. "You weren't kidding about beer in your fridge."

"Occasionally some of the guys from my group show up. It's all about hospitality."

She gave him the *yeah, right* look and he wondered if he should bother telling her he wasn't hooked on the beer, then decided *why bother?* They poured some coffee, then tried the granola bars.

"Do you think," Jazz asked, "that being made with yogurt makes a granola bar any healthier?"

"I dunno. I think of them as energy. Sugar."

She bit into hers. "Yup. I suppose there are enough good things in this to salve Iris's conscience."

He chuckled. "Jazz, she's an athlete. Lots of carbs required."

"That's true," she admitted. "I guess I'm thinking about my waistline and not hers."

He thought her waistline was just perfect but didn't embarrass her by saying so. One of those things better left unsaid unless a relationship became intimate. He switched tack.

"I've heard Iris mention her grandmother a few times, but I've never met her."

"You won't." Jazz sighed. "She's in a nursing home with full-blown Alzheimer's. She doesn't recognize Iris at all, and barely does any better with Lily or me."

"Now that is sad." His sympathy surged. "Not only sad, but awful."

"It is. My mind is so important to me that I can't imagine losing it. I'd hate it. Anyway, Mom is lost somewhere in her early life. She keeps asking for our dad who died ten years ago. She remembers Lily and me as small children and doesn't believe we're grown up now. She likes listening to the music of her era, and I visit as often as I can so she doesn't feel lonely."

"That's gotta be hard."

"It is, but with time I've gotten more used to it and just pretend I'm a friend. She can accept that."

"Ouch." Nothing to do, nothing to fix. Life's nastiest problems.

"Life can take some awful turns but I don't need to tell you that."

"I've got some buddies who suffered traumatic brain injuries." There he went, sharing again. "They're not much better off than your mom. And no, I'm not minimizing what's happening to you.

Just saying I kinda know what it's like from the outside looking in."

"I'm sure that's horrid, too. You still see the men and women they used to be."

"That's it."

After a minute or so, Jazz shook herself visibly. "God, when did I get morose? I'm not usually like this."

"The times aren't usual and I apologize for asking about your parents."

"Perfectly natural question." She waved a dismissive hand. "How long will it take those chops to thaw?"

"Not very. They're thin. Got any fresh brussels sprouts?"

"As a matter of fact, I do. Iris likes to eat them raw. Why?"

"I'll sauté them in butter. Scrumptious."

"That leaves her carbs." Jazz rested her chin in her hand. "Brown rice. For Iris, no other kind. Okay?"

He nodded. Distraction. This was all distraction, but she needed it. Come to that, so did he.

"I'll call the sheriff now," he announced. "A mug shot of the ex could be very helpful."

She nodded, her gaze still distant.

Gage reached for his cell, thinking he wouldn't blame Jazz if she wished she were back in Miami. A long, long way from this. Lily would no sooner have let her know this was going on than Jazz was telling Lily, even though Jazz had mentioned calling her sister a time or two.

But caught right in the middle was Iris which, given that Jazz was just her aunt, meant that Jazz was burdened with the question whether to tell Lily.

"Nothing's going to happen to Iris," Jazz announced firmly. "I'm not going to let it. I don't care about myself. I'll kill the bastard first anyway."

"That's obvious." Part of the conundrum, too. His heart squeezed as he thought of these two ladies who meant so much to him. But he had to let Jazz know. "Jazz, killing a man changes you forever. Don't do it if there's any way to avoid it."

Then he punched in the sheriff's number.

GAGE DALTON ARRIVED sooner than Jazz would have expected. She managed a smile and invited him in for coffee or a beer.

"I'll take that beer," he said. "Won't put me over the limit." He limped down the hall to the kitchen.

Two battle-scarred veterans, Jazz thought, even though she didn't know Gage's story.

"I heard you," Adam said, handing Gage a beer after he sat. "Welcome to the war room."

Gage lifted one brow. "The war room?"

"We're practically camped in here," Jazz answered. "We could go to the living room, though."

Gage shook his head. "Better with an upright back." He took a swig of beer. "Okay, you said something about a letter when you called?"

"I'll get it," Jazz said and jumped up. Any action, however small, felt necessary. She went into the office to pull down the envelope from the high shelf in the closet. The postcard was inside it.

Mutely she handed it to Gage, then leaned back against the counter, waiting.

"Department of Corrections," Gage read. "Oh, hell, don't tell me."

He pulled out the postcard first and read it aloud. "'I'm coming but you'll never know when.' Okay, that's taking the cake. This creep wants to keep Lily on tenterhooks."

Then he pulled the letter out of the envelope and scanned it. "Well, knock me down. This is almost impossible. I was checking into it, and even though Florida offers gain time to inmates who behave, it almost never gets applied. Some kind of crummy setup. I wonder how the hell this guy managed it?"

Jazz spoke. "I met Andy only a couple of times but the guy's a really smooth talker. I bet he got on the right person's good side."

"Must be." Gage ruminated briefly, then took another swig of beer. "Okay, I'll get a hold of this guy's booking photo or prison photo. I'll give it to every cop around. If he gets anywhere near here, someone should see him."

Adam spoke. "Only if they're looking in the right direction at the right time."

"Yeah, there is always that. And my people are spread pretty thin. So are the city police. They were just a sop to the egos of the city council. Not enough of them, really, to do all the policing in town."

He tapped the envelope on the desk. "I'll make this a priority. Mind if I take this letter? I'll return it, but there's information on it I need so there's no screwup on my end."

"Take it," Jazz said. "I'm not sure Lily will ever want to see it, but I guess she should."

"That's up to you, but I *will* return it."

Gage finished his beer and the two men hobbled to the front door. Jazz stayed put, hoping that at last they'd make some progress instead of spinning their wheels waiting for the next shoe to drop.

IN THE FIELD alongside the road, Andy Robbins hunkered down in the tall grasses waiting for Iris. In his hands he held an expensive camera, good cover for him. He'd found it in the truck and wondered if it was stolen, given the age and condition of that truck.

Probably. The idea amused him. Anyway, if anyone happened to stumble on him, he'd just say he was taking photos of the mountains.

Days lasted longer here, he noticed, than in Florida. The change in the lengths of the days wasn't hugely noticeable like it was here. Interesting and he wondered why but didn't care enough to find out.

Just as twilight took over from the brightness of day, he saw Iris come out of the community college gym. At first she was among a group of girls, but then she struck out on her own. That seemed odd, but he was glad of it.

He'd watch one more night after thinking about it, after finding a good place on that damn mountain. He wasn't used to mountains, and he didn't like the way they seemed to steal his breath.

He'd live. And he'd get what he wanted.

Smiling, he headed back to his camp, knowledge tucked away like seeds in a pinecone.

## Chapter Fourteen

Jazz waited for Iris to come home, nervous as always since the mess started. She couldn't help but worry about her niece, but agreed there was no point in trying to hem the girl in. She'd have plenty of reasons why that would be both awful and foolish, and Jazz didn't want to scare her. Clearly the threat was being directed at Lily.

Adam suggested they sit on the porch for a change of venue. "Nobody's going to come after you while I'm sitting right beside you."

She hesitated. "Gun?"

"I doubt it. This guy is more into scaring than shooting."

"Andy," she said. "Andy was like that."

"My guess is that prison didn't change him one bit."

"If it's him, then apparently not. But he did beat up Iris that one time."

As they moved to the porch with some instant

lemonade, mainly because Jazz couldn't face any more coffee, Adam didn't reply.

But once they were seated in the wooden rocking chairs out front with the ever-gentle Sheba beside Adam, he spoke.

"Sometimes I don't think prison changes anyone. Maybe it makes them worse. Regardless, he only attacked Iris that once, right?"

"Just the once."

"Then I doubt he wants to do it a second time. Mainly, from what you said, he wants control of Lily again, to put her in the same state of fear that he used during their marriage. Hurting Iris that first time only got him a trip to prison, not control of Lily."

She thought about it as she rocked, wishing the lemonade tasted as good as her mother's fresh-made. "You may be right," she allowed finally.

"Patterns. People always have patterns."

That was true. In her observation of people, used in her books, she had noted it but hadn't thought of it that way. People seldom changed. Change was hard, difficult. Ways of viewing things didn't much alter, either, though some would claim that they had. Usually, however, they just found a better reason for what they said and thought.

She sipped more lemonade, waving to a couple with a toddler who passed by on the sidewalk. This town felt so friendly to her and she hoped it wasn't an illusion.

"Twilight lasts so long here," she remarked. "It's shorter in Florida."

"We're farther north," he replied.

"I know, but the difference still surprises me. Longer evenings. Pleasant." But cool, too. She set her glass on the wooden table between them and pulled the gray cardigan closer around her front. Maybe she should have added another layer.

Boy, was she giving Lily's wardrobe a workout.

A man passed by, waving and calling a greeting to them by name. "Evening, Adam. Evening, Lily." He was truly dressed as a cowboy, Jazz noted with amusement. Common enough around here, she supposed, but she hadn't been out enough to notice.

She spoke. "Adam? You ever wear cowboy boots?"

"Only when I'm going to ride a horse, which isn't often. Dang things weren't designed for walking, although I suppose you could get used to them."

"What bothers you?"

"The heel. It's high and angled, designed to grip a stirrup. But when I'm walking, it shoves my feet down into the narrow toe box. Which is pointed to make it easier to slide into the stirrup."

She nearly laughed. "That's quite an analysis."

"I tried walking in them when I was younger. I figured out what was bothering me, that's all." He turned to look at her. "Now ropers are different, lower heel, rounder toes, tighter ankle. Better for roping cattle. Easier to walk in for long periods."

"That's the whole encyclopedia, I guess."

"Not hardly. There are different kinds of cowboy boots, too, but I don't want to bore you."

She doubted she would be bored, but why press him? Her concern about Iris was tightening around her, and she kept peering down the street hoping to see her niece.

"It's getting late. Iris should be home by now."

"Not that late," Adam answered. "We'll call out the cavalry if she doesn't appear soon."

How soon, she wondered. But just as she was considering calling for help, she saw Iris turn a corner and head toward them. Alone. Where were all the friends? she wondered as relief flooded her.

Iris waved, then trotted toward them. When she arrived at the porch steps, she grinned at Jazz. "Just can't stop worrying about me, Aunt Jazz?" Sheba jumped up to greet her and Iris rubbed her ears.

"I'm not used to being responsible for a girl your age," Jazz replied.

"Get used to it or you'll go crazy before Mom gets home. I'm gonna drop my bag inside then come join you guys. That's lemonade, right? No hidden shot of vermouth?"

"Iris!" But Jazz laughed. "It's not much of a lemonade, but it passes. The pitcher is on the counter."

"Be right back. Just don't start a romantic conversation. I'm not going to be long enough."

Romantic conversation? Jazz nearly blushed as she looked at Adam. He shrugged. "Not a bad idea, frankly."

*Not a bad idea?* Deep inside she thrilled to the words. Oh, God, no. She'd been trying to avoid these feelings almost since the outset, and now they were flooding her. She quickly looked away from Adam, fearing he might read her response in her eyes.

Iris returned in a couple of minutes. "Just flyers in the mail today. I ditched them," she remarked. "There's better lemonade than this?"

"Your grandmother used to make it. I tried a couple of times but I wasn't happy with the results. This is the best you'll get from me."

"Good enough." Iris drank half her glass. "Sally's avoiding me. Good."

"And the ex?"

"He doesn't matter to me anymore. He's a sleaze."

"Yup," was Jazz's only response. "Are you late home tonight?"

"Only because I dropped my backpack. I forgot to zip it. Papers everywhere, and it didn't help that it's breezy. The dog ate my homework ain't gonna fly."

Sheba nuzzled her then returned to Adam's side. Was Adam feeling bad? Jazz wondered. Nothing about him would indicate it, but he wasn't exactly smiling, either. And Sheba, who often seemed willing to abandon Adam for Iris, was almost clinging to him.

Maybe he was struggling with the memories he

so rarely mentioned. The thought saddened her and she wished she could help even though she was sure that there was no way. A man left in his own private hell, one which had no escape.

She had no idea how to reach out and get him to talk about it, either. As an introvert, starting a conversation, especially about difficult subjects, often eluded her. It was a good thing she didn't face the same problem in her books, she thought wryly. Or at least not often. Her characters were often splashed in bold colors, and when they weren't talking she could delve into their internal lives.

Not so in the real world.

She smothered a sigh at her own inadequacies. A sigh would have caused someone to ask her what was wrong, but what could she say? That she wished Adam would open up more, share his moody feelings?

Yeah, right.

At times she felt she knew him very well. At others he was a stranger. It would probably always be so.

As the twilight began to deepen, she shivered. It sure got cold quickly at this altitude. She rose, her nearly empty glass in hand. "This hothouse Florida girl is going inside to get warm."

Iris laughed at her. "Toughen up, Aunt Jazz."

"Not enough time to do that, kiddo. Don't give me a hard time. You two go ahead and enjoy yourselves out here."

Iris, Adam and Sheba followed her, however.

"Your dinner is in the microwave," Jazz told Iris. "I slaved all day over frozen ziti."

God, she loved to hear Iris laugh.

It wasn't long, however, before Iris cleaned up a large heap of the ziti and four pieces of garlic bread. She put her dishes in the dishwasher. "Bet that bread was frozen, too. I'm off!"

Then she ran upstairs presumably to phone and text friends.

Jazz arched a brow at Adam. "No homework?"

He'd pulled a longneck from the fridge and now sat at the table sipping the beer. "She's pretty diligent. I doubt she'd let that slide."

"You're right. She's an amazing girl."

"Not to put too fine a point on it." He stirred, shifting his weight on the chair.

She was immediately reminded of his pain and sympathy welled in her. "Would the living room be more comfortable?"

"Right now nothing would be."

"That's awful."

He shrugged.

She leaned forward. "Are you always so stoic?"

"What good would it do not to be? I'm lucky."

He'd said something like that before, but she wondered how often he didn't feel lucky at all. Not that he'd ever say.

But Sheba was plastered to his side, often looking up into his face. He petted her with his free hand, especially her long silky ears. Then he looked down at the dog. "Time for a walk?" he asked.

Sheba wagged her tail.

Adam looked at Jazz. "Just out back. Not a long one."

With those words he brought back the tension that had fled for just a little while when Iris returned safely home.

"I know," he said gently, as if he could read her face. "Nothing like walking down a narrow defile not knowing if the threat is above or below. Or even if it's there at all."

She nodded, wishing she could be braver. Sturdier. One thing for sure, she was getting angrier by the day. The taunting alone was cruel.

But if this did indeed turn out to be Lily's ex, she had a whole lot more to be angry about than that. She'd sat in court while her sister sat at the prosecutor's table and had listened to all of it. *All* of it.

She still couldn't imagine how hard it must have been for Lily to strip herself bare in court, talking about those matters. Admitting she had endured such things. Talking about the way she had been snared then terrified.

And the defense attorney! He was just doing his job, but trying to paint Lily as a liar? In the face of those X-rays and hospital reports? She wondered how anyone could stomach defending such a man.

Andy should just have pled guilty, but not Andy. As the trial progressed, she saw just how smarmy he was. Became certain that he believed he could charm his way out of anything.

But not that time.

Now, somehow, he must have charmed and smarmed his way into an early release. *Oh, I was the victim. That woman cheated on me, hated me and lied about me.* Or some such crap.

Sure.

Sighing, she put her head in her hands and stared at the tabletop. Now he was out there again, somewhere. Was he still a threat even after all this time?

But who else could it be? And how could he be found?

A shiver ran through her, but not from the cold. It wasn't a shiver of fear but felt more like her body was trying to release the unending tension. When Iris was around, Jazz played a role, as if everything was okay.

But nothing was okay, and she was certain she was taking another major shift in her world view. The biggest had been during the trial. This was a close second.

She hoped this bugger continued to mistake her for Lily and took his swipe at her. Anything to protect Lily and Iris. Anything.

"Please God," she murmured. "Let us finish this before Lily gets home. Before she has to become frightened, too."

At the moment, though, she wondered if God was even listening.

WALKING AROUND THE backyard with Sheba helped Adam as much as the dog. The grinding pain in his hip lessened a bit, and he enjoyed watching her sniff around. A dog's view must be so very different, and sometimes he wished he could experience that amazing sense of smell. It must paint the world in ways he couldn't imagine.

But at last Sheba finished her rounds. He cleaned up after her and carried the small bag to the trash bin.

He hadn't been this wound up in quite a while. He hated not being able to get a good grip on this threat, this man. All the guy had to do was make one mistake. Just one. So far he hadn't made a useful one if he'd made any at all.

If it *was* Andy Robbins seeking vengeance, he had to be a damn fool to come back for a second helping of Lily. People who allowed themselves to be driven by such things often screwed up. Got themselves into serious trouble. Made themselves too easy to identify.

He took Sheba back indoors and joined Jazz in the kitchen. How could he explain that the softness of the living room furniture aggravated his hip by bending it into different positions. He didn't like to talk about it, didn't want to seem like a complainer. But maybe, if Jazz asked again, he should tell her something about it.

Holding back all the time seemed stupid considering how much he liked her, how strongly he craved her. God, what a mess this had turned into.

He filled Sheba's bowl with fresh water, then asked, "Coffee? I need the caffeine to wash out the beer." Not strictly true but he needed to be on high alert.

"Sure," she answered, raising her head from her hands. "I feel like a tightly coiled spring anyway."

He studied her, his concern growing considerably. "You should skip the coffee and get some sleep."

"Nothing's going to let me sleep. Not yet. I'll just be alone in the dark worrying. It's nice to share that worry and have you buck me up."

Nice compliment, but overstated. "I haven't been doing much of that." When the coffee was ready, he poured two mugs and joined her at the table, easing into the chair. "This is like shadow boxing. Not nearly as satisfying as a punching bag."

She gave him a half smile. "I want to punch someone."

"Me, too."

"I can just hear Andy talking himself into an early release. He's so damned charming. Maintaining his innocence with sincerity. Blaming it all on Lily. I wonder if he believes that, too. But he *did* beat up Iris. For God's sake, Adam, she was just four."

He nodded and sipped his coffee. "A monster."

"At least."

"But none of these threats seem directed at Iris."

"Except maybe the flowers. *She* found them."

He didn't answer that one. There was no answer. They fell silent for a while.

Then Jazz jumped up. "I've got some of those frozen cinnamon buns. Whatever we don't eat will fuel Iris in the morning."

"Thanks. Sounds good with this coffee."

"I'm apt to put on ten pounds at this rate."

That wouldn't make her any less attractive. He believed nothing could do that.

More silence.

Then Jazz popped the question. "Tell me about your hip, *please*."

"I already told you the basics." But Adam knew that wasn't what she meant. He braced himself. He owed it to her, especially with what he was feeling about her. Besides, she'd take his secrets away with her when she flew home.

"War," he said after a few minutes. "Obviously. A rocket-propelled grenade from the cliffs above. Even though we were armored up, it blew a big hole in the transport. Those of us who could piled out to escape the fire. Then came the gunshots. American guns, stolen, or maybe some leftover Russian equipment. Armor-piercing bullets. They got a few of us, me included."

She paled, although clearly she couldn't imagine it. Who could unless they had been there?

"Oh my God," she murmured. "Sheer hell."

He couldn't deny that. But memories had begun to surface, making his skin crawl, his mind try to run into the past.

He decided to double down. If she couldn't handle it, then he needed to know before he dug himself in any deeper with her.

She pushed for it. "And now? It follows you?"

"Like too many people. It doesn't go away, Jazz. Apparently never. I carry a graveyard of faces inside me. The enemy, my buddies, they're all there."

He saw her eyes glisten with unshed tears.

"Don't ever kill anyone," he said slowly, for the second time. "It changes you forever."

She stared angrily at him. "Right now I'd like to."

"I imagine so."

"And the rest of it, Adam? Surely that's not all of it."

"It's not." He hesitated but remained determined to get through all of this. To learn her reaction even if it killed him inside.

He went to get more coffee, knowing he was trying to deflect the moment. *No go.*

Back at the table, he plunged in. "It haunts me all the time. It's always bubbling beneath the surface, trying to emerge. Sometimes it succeeds. I get angry, viciously angry, not fit to be around other people. I can withdraw entirely, facing it, reliving it. I run and work out trying to contain it, and most of the time that works. But not always. Talking about it at group can help, talking with others who have been there. But the issues never resolve. I'll be driving down the road, suddenly afraid of a roadside bomb. I wish I could find all my triggers, but I can't so I don't know how to avoid getting set off." He paused. "I can't ask anyone else to go through this with me."

She came around the table, wrapping her arm around his shoulders. "I'm so sorry, Adam. So sorry. But maybe instead of making that assumption you should ask, should try. Few of us are meant to go through life alone."

"I'm not alone," he answered stubbornly. But emotional intimacy? He was living without that all right.

Then he raised his head and looked up at her. In an instant everything clicked.

JAZZ FELT THE MOMENT. Something wild rose in her in answering the fire in his eyes. She wanted. She needed, and as everything else slipped away into the background, Adam rose and took her in his arms.

"Now," he said roughly.

"Now," she agreed.

Moments later they were in her bedroom, stripping wildly as if a hunger too long denied erupted into an explosion that blew them both away.

They tumbled onto the bed, hands seeking and exploring. Jazz felt as if there wasn't enough air in the entire universe as she silently begged for completion.

She reached down, surrounding his hardened staff with her fingers. The conflagration became consuming and she got her wish as he filled her, filled every corner of her body and soul.

She whispered his name, some part of her remembering Iris upstairs—that she didn't want to shock her niece. Then she climbed the roller coaster to the very top, and when she plunged over, her stomach feeling as if it had grown weightless, Adam followed her over the edge.

LATER IN A tangle of sheets and comforters, they lay tightly entwined. Jazz felt as if the glow that suffused her was brighter than the stars.

Adam spoke hoarsely. "I'm usually a better lover."

"Shh. It was great. No complaints."

"Someday…" He left the thought unfinished.

She didn't want to say the word. Her glow was fading, and as it seeped away, reality began to intrude. There would never be a someday. Their worlds were too far apart.

But reality also brought their biggest concern back to the forefront. Reluctantly they eased apart and reached for their clothes. Jazz didn't want even to risk a shower.

Danger lurked and it was growing closer.

THE NEXT EVENING, Andy Robbins snatched Iris. It was incredibly easy. She was alone, the twilight had begun to take over the world. He called her over to his truck saying he needed directions.

Iris came over as if she had nothing to fear in this world.

"Hey," he said when she reached his open window, "there's a fork ahead. Which way do I turn to reach the downtown?"

She smiled and opened her mouth to answer.

He grabbed her arm and at the same moment slapped the chloroformed rag over her mouth. Almost instantly she sagged.

He had her. Pushing her to one side, he slipped out of his truck, lifted her and hoisted her into the bed beneath the camper shell.

Nobody had seen. No one was around.

Satisfied by his own brilliance, he headed for the mountain nearby. Thunder Mountain he'd heard it called.

Now he really had something to hang over Lily's head. Something to terrify her once again into submission.

Behind him on the road lay Iris's backpack and sports duffel. No kind of trail for anyone to follow.

He began to whistle a jaunty tune.

## Chapter Fifteen

As the twilight eased toward night, Jazz was pacing, pacing until it was a wonder she hadn't worn a hole in Lily's rugs.

Adam had gone out to look for Iris, but the terror creeping along Jazz's spine worsened by the minute.

This was no case of an unzipped backpack. She tried to tell herself that Iris had fallen, sprained an ankle. Something so ordinary they could laugh about it later.

But she didn't believe it.

Then the landline phone rang. Her heart climbed into her throat.

"Hello?" Her voice shook.

A creepy voice came back, a voice Jazz had never forgotten, only this time it wasn't smarmy.

"I have my daughter," Andy Robbins said. "Don't call the police. I'd hate to have to hurt her like you made me do before. I'll call with instructions tomorrow morning. You'd better follow them to the letter, Lily, or you'll never see Iris again."

A click. The sound of an empty line.

She stood frozen, phone in hand, barely aware that Adam's truck had pulled up out front.

He nearly burst through the door, Sheba on his heels, carrying Jazz's backpack and duffel.

"Has she showed up?" he demanded.

Jazz shook her head. Violent tremors began to tear through her.

"I'm calling the police."

"No! Adam, no!"

He stopped, dropping Iris's things to the floor. "We've got to…"

"If we call the police Andy will hurt Iris."

His face darkened like a violent thunderstorm. "That bastard. That bastard!"

"He'll do it, Adam. He's done it before."

That froze him. His face darkened even more if that was possible. "I take it he called."

She nodded and her tremors worsened. She felt on the verge of collapse. Her mind rebelled but the sound of Andy's voice in her head wouldn't let her escape. The worst nightmare had become real.

Adam came to her and wrapped her tightly in his arms. "We're going to get through this. We'll get Iris back safely."

She shook her head and tried to back out of his embrace. "You can't know that."

He didn't argue. "I suppose he'll call with instructions? When?"

She spoke, her voice shaking. "Morning? He said

he'd call but I'm not sure when. I don't know if I can stand the waiting. All I can think of is Iris out there, terrified, in the grip of a maniac."

The image was too vivid.

ADAM KNEW HIS own capabilities. Capabilities this animal wasn't considering. Reluctantly, he released Jazz. She hugged herself instead. He'd have cut off his own head to save her and Iris, but she didn't need to hear that. It wouldn't help.

"Let's go to our command center," he said.

"Our what?"

"The kitchen. Where we do everything."

He'd hoped for even a small smile but didn't get it.

"I don't know if I can hold still," she answered.

"Try it. We need to clear our heads."

As if that was going to be easy for either of them.

He made the inevitable coffee, forgoing a beer because he didn't want his head even the tiniest bit clouded.

But clear thought wouldn't come immediately. They were both too worried, preoccupied by their fears for Iris.

"I'm so upset about Iris," Jazz said presently. "So worried. My God, if we get her back safely, how is this going to affect her? She won't be the same bubbly girl anymore."

He wanted to disagree but couldn't. An experience like this had to have an impact, even if she and

Lily and Jazz were all unharmed. Maybe that was the thing that made him angriest of all: what this would do to all of them even with the best outcome.

Sheba nudged his thigh, then laid her head on it. He absently stroked her silky ears and fought back the memories that this tension summoned. Not the time for that. Not now.

He and Jazz were stuck waiting for the next move.

ANDY ROBBINS FELT extremely proud of himself. No one had seen him grab the girl, although by now they'd found her backpack and duffel, which would only heighten Lily's fear. Good. Let her stew in it.

Equally pleasing was the way Iris had given him no trouble. The chloroform had steadily worn off while she was in the back of his truck and, though she was still woozy, she'd followed his every direction as they climbed the mountain after leaving his truck behind. The way Lily once had. The way Lily would do again.

He carried a backpack of additional supplies for the girl. He didn't want her to go hungry or become dehydrated and he didn't know for sure how long this might take. He was a good father, after all, despite what Lily had claimed in court.

Well, he'd make sure Iris was safe in the cave he'd found just for her. It wasn't big, but he'd tie her so she could get around and move when she needed to. He'd already stashed some food and blankets up there.

Yeah, he was a good dad.

He didn't whistle on the way up the mountain. The climb left him somewhat breathless, as it would Lily. He smiled at the thought.

And behind him, the girl walked obediently. Not even teenage mouthiness. She'd figured out who was boss and didn't argue.

Lily would figure it out, too. The only question was how long he would make her suffer.

THE NIGHT WAS ENDLESS, swamped with terrible fear and anguish. Jazz's head filled with horrific ideas of what that man might do to Iris. Another, worse, beating? Rape? Leaving her alone somewhere cold and frightened in the dark, hungry and thirsty?

Andy was capable of all that. Andy was capable of just about anything. His desire to inflict suffering knew no bounds and while he had said he wouldn't hurt Iris if Lily followed his directions, she feared he'd been lying about that as he'd lied about everything in his life.

She paced endlessly, cold to the bone. No sweater could ease this aching chill.

Every time she looked at Adam, she saw her fears reflected, although in a different way. The man looked hard, his face almost like stone and his eyes…those kind brown eyes were almost black. He'd kill. She knew he'd kill Andy.

Good riddance to scum, she thought. Good riddance.

Until she recalled how Adam had said that killing someone changed you forever. Oh, God, don't let it come to that. He was carrying enough ghosts for an entire army.

But she sure as hell wouldn't blame him.

At last she got herself another cup of coffee. Maybe it would help warm her, and Adam had kept the pot fresh all night.

God, when had mere minutes become so endless?

At last she sagged at the table across from him. He shifted, easing his hip. Sheba slept in a corner by the cupboards but every time something moved, her eyes opened. A very light sleep. The tension in this house must be troubling her, but what could Jazz do about it?

"I feel like a coiled spring," she said.

Adam nodded. "That's one description. I'm feeling murderous."

She had guessed it. How uncomfortable that must be making him feel. How many bad memories this must be dredging out of him.

She ached for him, too. Andy was messing them all up.

"We'll get through this," he said, his voice as tight as stretched steel. "Swear to God."

She shivered, thinking that no one should want to cross this man. No one.

IRIS TREMBLED IN the cave when she'd been left, tied to a nearby tree with sturdy climbing rope. Her father—God, her own *father*—was doing this. Yeah, she knew who he was. Recognition had exploded within her out of the nearly forgotten past. *Her father.*

Something about that man had made her reluctant to fight, choosing patience instead, seeking any kind of opportunity to escape. She hadn't found one.

When the creep left her in the dark cave, she wasn't at all impressed by the water he'd left her, or the packages of power bars. They didn't reassure her.

Instead she felt around hoping to find a rock sharp enough to cut the rope that bound her. She had no idea where she could go if she escaped. Wandering around on this mountain without guidance could kill people.

He'd left her a musty, filthy blanket. She pulled it around herself against the night's cold, her mind whirling with useless ideas.

He'd promised he wouldn't hurt her. He just wanted her mother. She didn't believe him.

Iris started praying for Lily more than herself. For Jazz who was facing all of this.

Hoping that Adam would find a way to get to her. Her only real hope.

Maybe in the morning, with some light, she'd have better ideas. Then her mind drifted into happier places, so many wonderful times with her mother, so many good ones with Aunt Jazz. Great times with her friends.

She'd been blessed. Only now did she realize just how blessed.

WITH DAWN THE horror remained. Jazz felt as if she were stretched to breaking, but snapping would help nothing. Sleep might have helped, but she was well past that. Adrenaline would keep her going until she collapsed.

She tried to tell herself she was being ridiculous, that when the phone rang she'd instantly emerge from the deepest sleep, that she couldn't do anything until Andy told her what he wanted.

That didn't help. Worry crawled through her and all over her skin like a million stinging ants.

It was after ten when the phone finally rang. Adam was right there with her. She picked up the handset and heard the line crackling.

Andy was on a cell phone, the signal poor in the mountains. From that she knew he had Iris in the rugged, higher terrain, a terribly vast space, impossible to search in any timely fashion.

Her heart and stomach sank until she wondered if she might vomit.

"Lily."

She'd never forgotten that voice, not after the trial. "I'm here. If you hurt my daughter—"

"She's my daughter, too."

That oily voice sickened her even more. As if Iris's relationship to him had ever mattered to Andy.

"Now listen," he said.

"I'm listening."

"You drive up the dirt road leading to the old mining town. Then hike northwest and start climbing. On foot. I'll see you. I'll let you know where I want you to go. But hear me, and don't mistake me. If you call the cops, if you bring anyone along on the hike, I may just forget Iris is my daughter. God, what a stupid name."

Then he disconnected, leaving nothing but the hum of an empty line.

Jazz looked at Adam, her torment reaching new levels.

"I heard," he said coldly.

"He'll kill me," Jazz said quietly. "Worse, he might kill Iris."

"I know. I'll come anyway."

Anger burst in her, a white-hot heat. "Don't you dare. I mean it. I'm not risking Iris, not for your male ego."

He looked as if she'd slapped him but then the icy expression returned. "I get it."

"I mean it," she repeated. "There's nothing you can do to help now."

"I can fill a light backpack for you. You'll probably need some water, maybe even some trail mix. Climbing in the mountains can wear you out quickly, make you easy prey."

She shuddered but let him help her fill a pack she had seen in Lily's bedroom. Those water bottles would be heavy, but she didn't care. If she could have shaken the mountains, she would have.

She let Adam drive her to the mining camp, then set out alone, wrapped in a thicker jacket of Lily's, carrying gloves in her pockets along with a small canister in one, and a compass in her hand.

Northwest. Even that was a huge area.

Adam gave her a tight hug before he drove away, leaving her all alone to face the unimaginable.

EXCEPT ADAM DIDN'T leave her alone. He had no intention of doing that. The situation was too unstable, too dangerous, to leave Jazz out there on her own. Or to rely on Andy Robbins to reveal Iris's whereabouts in any useful way to rescue the girl.

And if there was one certainty in the middle of this mess, it was that Andy Robbins didn't have Adam's ability to track stealthily from a distance.

He drove off a side road that headed south not much below the remains of the small mining town. He had a survival pack in the rear of his truck, an army habit he hadn't been able to break. Thank God.

Shortly he was outfitted in camo, a pair of high-powered thermal binoculars hanging around his neck and his rifle slung over his right shoulder.

He had a decent idea of where Andy had put Iris. The compass direction given to Jazz had been a big clue to Adam.

Thunder Mountain protected a wolf den, a small cave that had somehow escaped the crushing weight above it. Andy would have chosen that, not an unprotected open space where Iris might be more easily found. A place where he could pretend that he was protecting his daughter. As if.

Adam wasn't worried about the small pack of wolves up there. They were shy creatures and if their pups weren't inside, they'd stay back, watching. Waiting to take their home back. The den was essential to the pack's survival as a group, but not essential enough to risk a battle with a human predator. *Their* larger prey were mostly grazing animals that offered a threat only with their heels. Wolves were far smarter than the humans they dodged. Never fighting a battle that wasn't essential, never starting a war.

The climb over rough ground was riddled with the cuts and gorges created by runoff from the winter snows and the remaining glaciers above. He climbed through obstacles as much as he moved through gentler ground.

He ignored the agonizing pain in his hip that was growing almost with each step. And frequently he paused, seeking Jazz's heat signature between trees.

He still had her in his sights, but no sign of Andy. How far was that bastard going to make her climb? How many risks would he put her through, maybe hoping she'd hurt herself and he'd have her under his full control?

From time to time, Adam searched other directions, taking no chance the monster would come at her from the side.

Not that he believed that bastard was capable of that kind of caution. If the fool had possessed a brain, he'd have known that you don't threaten a mama bear's cub.

Adam had even managed to press a can of pepper spray in Jazz's pocket. She'd looked at it, then nodded.

Adam was sure she'd burn out Andy's eyes if she got the chance. He just hoped she'd be upwind if she used that stuff.

But she would be too furious to think about it. He hadn't offered a caution because he knew that if the opportunity came Jazz wouldn't consider any such thing. She'd gone long past protecting herself.

Gritting his teeth against pain, he continued his trek. He knew where Jazz was. He just wished he knew Andy's position.

ANDY LAY CONCEALED behind a boulder, watching Lily's hike through binoculars. He'd seen that guy drop her off and head back home. Good.

The only question on his mind now was just how much he was going to make that woman suffer for all she'd done to him. Because she *was* going to suffer. His payback for all the pain she had caused him. He deserved it, just as she deserved the hell he intended to put her through.

She'd be on her knees begging before he was done. She'd be promising him anything at all if he would let Iris go. He liked that picture and began to grow impatient.

As for Iris, he planned to take her with him. He was her father, dammit. He needed to raise her right: obedient, wanting to please him. A *true* woman. She was still young enough to be molded into what Lily should have been.

Savoring the images that had begun to grow in his mind's eye, he counseled himself to patience.

Look at Lily now, he thought. Climbing as ordered. Being a good woman at last.

JAZZ DEVELOPED A new worry as she climbed along a narrow game trail. Hours now and no sign of Andy. Did he intend to take Iris away and begin his own form of in-home schooling? If she'd had the strength left to shiver, she would have. Instead she kept putting one foot in front of the other.

Two hours. She'd been climbing for over two hours now. Physical fatigue began to overwhelm her. She'd have to sit, wasting precious minutes drinking water, eating one of those power bars Adam had tucked in her pack. No choice.

At last she found a deadfall with one trunk about the right size to sit on. If she didn't keep her strength up, she might never climb high enough.

She wasn't used to this new altitude and she could feel her lungs protesting, her cells kicking her with their need for more oxygen. Too bad. She *had* to keep going. Every minute she rested was causing Iris more terror, more suffering.

But life in the gentler landscape of Florida hadn't prepared her for this treacherous terrain. So much of it, so endless.

She wished she'd brought a pistol because she'd delight in shooting Andy, but she also knew she probably wouldn't have had the chance to use it. Or maybe even the will.

But what he was doing to Iris…

She rose, grabbing the backpack. She *had* to get going again.

ADAM SAW JAZZ SIT, saw her get up after a few minutes. He swept the entire area around her once again. Nothing, dammit. Nothing.

Then he caught a heat signature a few hundred yards above Jazz. His quarry. He set out, trusting the duff to cover his sounds, moving as lightly as he ever had in a battle zone. Creeping up on the enemy. It was in his blood.

The shrieking in his hip acted as a goad.

Nothing would stop him now.

ANDY ENJOYED WATCHING Lily struggle up the mountain. The woman was soft, too used to a desk job. He'd used his prison time to get into the best shape of his life.

Poor little woman. She had no idea of the hell that

was coming her way. No real idea. If she thought
he'd been hard on her before, she had no idea how
hard he could get. He'd practically been a pussycat
before prison. No more.

Unable to wait any longer, sure that Lily was alone,
he got going. It was high time. He'd waited ten long
years for this.

ADAM WAS SWINGING around behind Andy. The ele-
ment of surprise couldn't be overrated. Andy would
be focused on Lily and not expecting a rear attack.
The coming moves were already clear in Adam's
mind. He just needed to be able to protect Jazz before the creep could harm her.

He'd make it.

JAZZ HEARD ANDY COMING. He didn't even try to be
quiet about it. Confident brute.

But maybe he had every right to be. He'd kid-
napped Iris. He'd forced Jazz to come up alone into
these mountains. But she had to find Iris. Get that man
to take her to her niece. Whatever the cost to herself.

She just had to hope that some opportunity would
come to kick the guy in his package or scratch his
eyes out. Or get that pepper spray out of her pocket
and use it.

Andy's voice, smarmy again said, "Hello, Lily.
Ready to fall back in line?"

"I loved you once," Jazz said.

"You'll love me again. Drop that backpack."

She did as ordered, then said, "If you want me you're going to have to take me to Iris."

"All in good time. Don't move. I didn't come to this party unarmed. I can gut you like I did to that squirrel."

Fury and fear both filling her, she stood still. He came around behind her, grabbed her hands and began to tie them together.

She thought of snapping her head back to hit him in the mouth or chin but stopped herself. That wouldn't get her to Iris.

Then she caught sight of the slightest movement in the brush above.

Adam! Oh my God, Adam.

ADAM HAD TO alter his tactic. Andy was now behind Jazz. To come from behind, he'd have to swing around a bit.

Easy enough. Plans were made to be adjusted.

He moved, taking care not to dislodge anything with his boots, creeping as silently as he'd ever crept in the 'Stan.

ANDY SPOKE, FOR once not trying to charm. "My knife is right against your back. You might not feel it with that jacket on, but that doesn't make any difference. It'll slice through and get you in the spine. Now *climb*!"

Jazz did as directed, just as she was sure Iris had. Some risks were foolhardy, and with her wrists bound the chance of getting at Andy seemed impossible.

She thought of Iris being forced up here the same way, and she coiled with anger, hating her helplessness.

But Adam was out there somewhere. He hadn't listened to her, and so far Andy seemed to suspect nothing.

Her only hope now. Iris's only hope. She clung to it as her weary legs continued to climb. Prayed Adam wouldn't do a thing that might endanger Iris.

ADAM HAD NEARLY reached the best position, grateful for the brush that concealed his movements. The undergrowth had begun to green with spring, making it quieter when he moved through it.

Andy and Jazz passed him. He waited another minute for his best opportunity. Bound like that, a knife behind her, meant Jazz couldn't do a damn thing to help.

And he had to get to Andy before he cut her.

His breathing slowed. The pain in his hip seemed to vanish. He was as still and silent inside as he'd been on any covert operation.

He saw his opportunity and got ready to spring with his rifle in his hands. He'd have just liked to shoot the SOB but couldn't risk the possibility that he might be wrong about where Iris was stashed.

Then his moment came and he leaped onto the game trail right behind Andy.

Jazz heard the wonderful voice say, "I've got the business end of this rifle on your back, Robbins. Stop or I'll shoot you now."

Andy started to turn. "You'll shoot Lily, too."

"My aim is better than that. Stop now. Let Jazz get ahead of you or you'll take your last breath."

Jazz? Confounded, Andy let Lily go ahead. There was no mistaking the rifle pressed hard into his back. Jazz? Lily's sister?

The rifle prodded him. "Drop that knife. Then get facedown. Now."

Not even Andy was stupid enough to try to argue with a rifle. He valued his hide more than revenge, and the steadiness of the icy voice behind him warned him that this man knew what he was doing.

He dropped the knife, watched a tan boot kick it beyond reach.

"Facedown," the steely voice said. "I know a hundred ways to disable or kill a man."

Andy didn't doubt it. Beaten, he lay down, his face full of dirt. A heavy boot landed on his back and he let his wrists be bound tightly.

"Jazz? Come over here."

She obeyed. Andy heard a knife saw through the rope around her wrists.

"Take us to Iris now." A hand gripped Andy beneath his shoulder, pulling him to his feet as if he weighed nothing. "*Now* or you're going to look like something that the butcher has ground for sausage."

Jazz watched all this with amazement. Adam had spoken those words and she never doubted he'd meant them. Would Andy really take them to Iris? He'd certainly looked cowed.

The trail resumed its steady upward march. Her legs burned and started to feel weak, but thoughts of Iris kept her going.

Then at last they emerged into a small clearing and found Iris trying to cut through a rope with a sharp rock.

When Jazz saw her she collapsed with relief. And Iris cried, "I've never been so happy to see anyone in my life!"

Hugging each other, she and Iris stumbled after Andy and Adam, back down toward the mining camp.

"Try your cell," Adam said to Jazz. "Dial 911 and keep at it until you get a signal."

Finally she found one, about the time they reached the decrepit mining town. They sat at last and the two women started to cry.

"We'll wait for rescue," Adam said. "Best day of my life."

"Mine, too," Iris and Jazz sobbed in unison.

The best day indeed.

After a sheriff's deputy arrived and carted Andy away in cuffs, Adam led the way to his truck.

He stashed their gear in the back, thrilled they had Iris back. And sorry Jazz had seen the worst side of him. The pain pierced his heart.

## Chapter Sixteen

Jazz didn't call her sister. She figured Lily didn't need to get upset until she was home in a few days, able to see Iris safe.

Iris huddled in the recliner, wrapped in a blanket, still trying to process the horror she's experienced, accepting endless cups of cocoa, her appetite otherwise diminished.

How was her niece going to deal with this, Jazz wondered. Another psychologist? Probably.

Andy resided safely in the county jail. He'd probably face federal charges as well as state and county. She hoped that would make Iris and Lily safe for much longer than ten years.

But Adam had not reappeared. He'd turned his truck into his own driveway after helping Iris and Jazz inside and hadn't been to see them since.

Jazz hated to imagine the memories this event had stirred in him, turning him into a man who had stalked a killer and had made dire threats.

A man who had once again turned into the very thing he'd been trying to escape.

Her heart bled for him and she shed tears for him.

After two days, she decided it was enough. Risking everything, risking seeing him caught up in PTSD, she asked Iris if she'd be all right for an hour or so.

Iris nodded. "Sure."

*Sure.* Not very comforting.

Then Jazz screwed up her determination and marched across the street. She had to knock several times before Adam answered the door.

He looked awful, unshaven, wearing his rumpled camo as if he hadn't changed clothes. His face was drawn into harsh lines, his color faded to gray. Sheba looked saddened.

He let her in reluctantly, but said, "Go home, Jazz. Iris needs you."

"She's not the only one."

"Ms. Mercy marching across the street, huh? Go home. You've seen some of the worst in me. I don't want you to see any more."

She stared at him, wondering what the hell she could do. Then she did the only thing she could think of.

Closing the space between them, she wrapped her arms around him and hugged him as tight as she could. He stiffened.

"Jazz…"

"Shut up, Adam. I'll love you any way you come."

He froze. "You don't know."

"I know now, and I was never so grateful for a warrior. I've got a good idea what you might have done out there. I don't care. I still love you. Will always love you. Get as angry as you want. Hide away when you need to. Run on that lousy hip for hours. I've also seen the best in you."

His stiffness began to ease. "You can't know."

"Maybe not all of it, but I'll deal with it as it comes. Because I love you."

He moved back just enough to look into her face. "You really mean that?" He sounded tentative now.

"I really mean that. I wouldn't say it if I didn't."

"God, Jazz!"

"How many times do I have to say it to get it through that thick skull of yours? If you can tell me you don't feel the same, that you just want me to go back to Miami, tell me now. Send me away into the loneliness without you. It'll practically kill me, but you don't need to worry about that."

His face at last softened completely. "I can't send you back to Miami."

"Well, good. We can sort everything else out later. I love you," she repeated for the umpteenth time.

A frown flickered across his features. "You've got to promise me you'll hang around to see more of this, and I don't mean a week or two. And that you'll leave anytime you can't take it."

Her heart began to take wing as he spoke, however indirectly, about a future. "I promise."

Then he smiled, like the sun rising on a gray day. "I love you, too. But give it time. Now let's take Sheba back to Iris. She needs the dog more than I do now. But not as much as I need you."

The usually silent Sheba woofed.

It was settled, Jazz thought as Adam's arms cradled her gently. So good. It would always be good even on the darkest of days.

Because she trusted him completely. Because he now owned her heart.

Then she began to smile, too.

\* \* \* \* \*

*Don't miss other romances in Rachel Lee's thrilling Conard County: The Next Generation series:*

Conard County: Christmas Bodyguard
Conard County: Traces of Murder
Conard County: Hard Proof
Conard County Justice
Stalked in Conard County
Murdered in Conard County

*Available now from Harlequin Books!*

# WE HOPE YOU ENJOYED
## THIS BOOK FROM

### ⊕ HARLEQUIN

# INTRIGUE

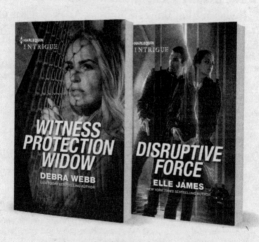

*Seek thrills. Solve crimes. Justice served.*

---

Dive into action-packed stories that will keep you
on the edge of your seat. Solve the crime
and deliver justice at all costs.

**6 NEW BOOKS AVAILABLE EVERY MONTH!**

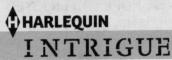
## #2061 MURDER GONE COLD
### A Colt Brothers Investigation • by B.J. Daniels
When James Colt decides to solve his late father's final murder case, he has no idea it will implicate his high school crush Lorelei Wilkins's stepmother. Now James and Lorelei must unravel a cover-up involving some of the finest citizens of Lonesome, Montana...including a killer determined to keep the truth hidden.

## #2062 DECOY TRAINING
### K-9s on Patrol • by Caridad Piñeiro
Former marine Shane Adler's used to perilous situations. But he's stunned to find danger in the peaceful Idaho mountains—especially swirling around his beautiful dog trainer, Piper Lambert. It's up to Shane—and his loyal K-9 in training, Decoy—to make sure a mysterious enemy won't derail her new beginning...or his.

## #2063 SETUP AT WHISKEY GULCH
### The Outriders Series • by Elle James
After losing her fiancé to an IED explosion, sheriff's deputy Dallas Jones planned to start over in Whiskey Gulch. But when she finds herself in the middle of a murder investigation, Dallas partners with Outrider Levi Warren. Their investigation, riddled with gangs, drugs and death threats, sparks an unexpected attraction—one they may not survive.

## #2064 GRIZZLY CREEK STANDOFF
### Eagle Mountain: Search for Suspects • by Cindi Myers
When police deputy Ronin Doyle happens upon stunning Courtney Baker, he can't shake the feeling that something's not right. And as the lawman's engulfed by an investigation that rocks their serene community, more and more he's convinced that Courtney's boyfriend has swept her—and her beloved daughter—into something sinister...

## #2065 ACCIDENTAL WITNESS
### Heartland Heroes • by Julie Anne Lindsey
While searching for her missing roommate, Jen Jordan barely survives coming face-to-face with a gunman. Panicked, the headstrong mom enlists the help of Deputy Knox Winchester, her late fiancé's best friend, who will have to race against time to protect Jen and her baby...and expose the criminals putting all their lives in jeopardy.

## #2066 GASLIGHTED IN COLORADO
### by Cassie Miles
Deputy John Graystone vows to help Caroline McAllister recover her fractured memories of why she's covered in blood. As mounting evidence surrounds Caroline, a stalker arrives on the scene shooting from the shadows and leaving terrifying notes. Is John protecting—and falling for—an amnesiac victim being gaslighted...or is there more to this crime than he ever imagined?

Saturday evening the crows came. Jasper Cole looked up from where he'd been standing in his ranch kitchen cleaning up his dinner dishes. He'd heard the rustle of feathers and looked up with a start to see several dozen crows congregated on the telephone line outside.

Just the sight of them stirred a memory of a time dozens of crows had come to his grandparents' farmhouse when he was five. The chill he felt at both the memory and the arrival of the crows had nothing to do with the cool Montana spring air coming in through the kitchen window.

He stared at the birds, noticing that they all seemed to be watching him. There were so many of them, their ebony bodies silhouetted against a cloudless sky, their shiny dark eyes glittering in the growing twilight. As this murder of crows began to caw, he listened as if this time he might decode whatever they'd come to tell him. But like last time, he couldn't make sense of it. Was it another warning, one he was going to wish that he'd heeded?

Laughing to himself, he closed the window and finished his dishes. He didn't really believe the crows were a portent of what was to come this time—any more than last time. His grandmother had, though. He remembered watching her cross herself and mumble a prayer as if the crows were an omen of something sinister on its way. As it turned out, she'd been right.

At almost forty, Jasper could scoff all he wanted, even as a bad feeling settled deep in his belly. That feeling only worsened as the crows suddenly all took flight as if their work was done.

Over the next few days, he would remember the evening the crows appeared. It was the same day Leviathan Nash arrived in Buckhorn, Montana, to open his shop in the old carriage house and strange things had begun to happen—even before people started dying.

*Don't miss*
Before Buckhorn *by B.J. Daniels,*
*available February 2022 wherever*
*HQN books and ebooks are sold.*

HQNBooks.com

PHBJDEXP0222

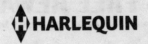 **HARLEQUIN**

*Heartfelt or thrilling, passionate or uplifting—Harlequin is more than just happily-ever-after.*

With twelve different series to choose from and new books available every month, you are sure to find stories that will move you, uplift you, inspire and delight you.

## SIGN UP FOR THE HARLEQUIN NEWSLETTER

Be the first to hear about great new reads and exciting offers!

### Harlequin.com/newsletters